MATERIAL EVIDENCE

Who would want to steal a corpse and why?

Jack Trombetta

PUBLISHING

The opinions expressed by the author are not necessarily those of 55:11 Publishing LLC.
Published by 55:11 Publishing LLC
1701 Walnut Street 7th Floor | Philadelphia, Pennsylvania 19103
USA
info@5511publishing.com| www.5511publishing.com
55:11 Publishing is committed to *Publishing with Purpose*. The company reflects the philosophy established by the founders, based on Isaiah 55:11:
"So is my word that goes out from my mouth: it will not return to me empty, but will accomplish what I desire and achieve the purpose for which I sent it."
Book design copyright © 2013 by 55:11 Publishing LLC. All rights reserved.
Cover design by Tim Janicki, Sight2Site Media, www.s2smedia.net
Published in the United States of America
ISBN: 978-0-9838517-2-1
1. Fiction:General:Historical
2. Fiction:Mystery/Detective:Historic.

Dedication

To my beloved nephew who inspired me to write this book.

John David Maher, Jr.
9/12/77—12/15/05

In your name I praise
For it was Christ who was raised
To deliver me from sin
So a new life I could begin
Dear Jesus, make my path straight
Until the day I see those Pearly Gates
With love I shall patiently wait
For what you did for me is truly great
All Praise to my Lord
And Savior Jesus Christ
Who embodied my sin
So I shall live everlasting
John D. Maher, Jr.

Acknowledgements

Thanks for their love and support.

My wife Lynn and children Joseph, Gina, and Jack. My
church family for their prayers.
Jeff Lindsey for his legal assistance and prayers.
Cherri Olsen for her advice and editing.
All my family too numerous to mention individually.

Foreword

Many times over the years, my friend and colleague, retired Detective Commander Jack Trombetta, would picture himself in biblical times and discuss how he may have responded to many of the challenges and dilemmas Christ's disciples and followers faced. Jack's magnetic personality and vivid imagination have taken listeners on many an adventure into the lives of the Apostles.

In *Material Evidence* Trombetta uses his twenty-five years of experience as a police officer and criminal investigator to take the reader back in time to the crucifixion of Jesus Christ. Through the character of Marcus, a Roman centurion, Trombetta conducts a criminal investigation of the death of Jesus and the disappearance of his body from the tomb. An adept investigator and interviewer, Jack reveals to the reader his passion for Christianity and his expertise in human relations and understanding. Through Marcus's relationship with his associate, Anthony, Trombetta portrays the struggles that we all may have as we balance faith, the historical record of Christ, and our human weakness and frailties.

Centurion Marcus's investigation becomes a quest to find out, *who is this Jesus?*

If you're looking for spiritual truth, you need to read *Material Evidence*. Retired Detective Jack Trombetta answers all the theories about the death and resurrection of the Lord Jesus Christ. He establishes the historical record and shows the only reasonable conclusion. Marcus's investigation plants more than a seed of possibility for the mystery of the empty tomb.

If you are a Christian and want to learn more about the biblical record of prophesies pointing to Christ, you need to read *Material Evidence*. Understanding the references made over hundreds of years by various biblical authors about the day that Christ was crucified will excite the believer and strengthen his or her faith. Material Evidence is more than a fictional novel; it provokes the reader toward a personal conviction on the person and work of Jesus Christ.

John D. Maher
Chief of Police (ret)
Lower Township Police Department
Cape May County, New Jersey

MATERIAL EVIDENCE

Pilate's Order

Gazing out his terrace toward the Jewish Temple, Pilate said, "This has been a very stressful and disturbing week, Demetrios. I don't remember a time when I have felt so vulnerable. It seems I've lost control of these events, as if the gods have turned their backs on me."

Turning to the servant, Pilate went on, "I need you to run an errand for me. Make your way to the gymnasium and locate the Centurion Marcus. He should be there with his partner, Anthony. He will not be hard to find. He is the head instructor and is always practicing and teaching war tactics. Advise him that I request his presence immediately. Don't give him any specifics concerning the missing prisoner. Tell him to make his way to the palace and report to me."

"As you wish," replied Demetrios, inclining his head in a respectful bow. "However, it would be my honor to investigate this crime against the empire, your Highness. I will hunt down the criminals and give you their heads on a plate."

"Oh, that is very funny, Demetrios," Pilate snorted. "I think Herod appreciates heads on a plate. I remember a few years ago he did just that very thing to a Jewish troublemaker." Furrowing his brow and pursing his lips,

Pilate added, "I believe he, too, was a follower of this Jesus of Nazareth. Was his name not John the baptizer?"

As he looked at Demetrios, Pilate thought, *What a loyal and dutiful servant he has been. I have always had great success with the Greek slaves; they are a sturdy tribe and eloquent in thought and speech. One day I will give him his freedom.*

Aloud, Pilate said, "I appreciate your zeal, Demetrios. However, Marcus has a tremendous amount of expertise in dealing with these Jews. I have known him since he was a boy, and the man has turned into a great warrior for the empire. But more important than this is his knowledge of Jews and their belief system. He has been trained for such an assignment. He has put the empire's money to good use, establishing a network of contacts in the Jewish community. This has been invaluable in keeping them in check and predicting their next move. The Jews are a very rebellious people, and we must always be a step ahead of them. In fact, it was Marcus's information that made it possible to squash that Jewish rebellion and arrest the notorious murderer Barabbas."

At the mention of Barabbas, Demetrios knew the conversation was at an end.

Barabbas was a bitter subject to the governor. Pilate had failed to anticipate the crowd's request to spare the life of the infamous enemy of Rome, and he had been astounded by their condemnation of the quiet carpenter from Nazareth.

Demetrios bowed deeply from his waist, spun on his heels, and left the governor brooding over these matters.

Demetrios saddled his horse, of which he was very proud. The gift of this fine animal from Pontius Pilate indicated the governor's esteem. Ordinarily, a servant would have had to run the five-mile distance to the gymnasium, located north of the Jewish Temple.

The buildings in the Judean province had been placed in specific order by King Herod the Great, a ruthless and cruel ruler but a famous architect of massive building projects. Dead for almost three decades, he was the father of the present Herod Antipas, beheader of the baptizer.

Upon Herod's death, Judea had been divided between his three sons, Herod Antipas, Archelaus, and Herod Philip, who ruled the province as tetrarchs. The Roman Senate had not declared them "kings" of the Jews, a title the senators had conferred only upon their father. As a young man, Herod the Great had gained the favor of Julius Caesar and Mark Anthony when he had proven himself a fierce warrior and strong ally to Rome in the battle for empire against Greece.

King Herod had placed the Roman garrison alongside the Jewish Temple. It was his thought that if any rebellion would take place in his province it would likely occur in the Jewish quarter. Farther north he had built the gymnasium for the soldiers' training. It was important to have a well-equipped and well-trained force to deal with all potential problems.

• • •

As Demetrios entered the gym he was overwhelmed with the vastness and the workmanship. Everywhere he looked he observed soldiers practicing the art of war. Peering to the east of the building he noticed two soldiers instructing a contingent of several dozen in the proper use of their shields when under attack by enemy arrows.

Approaching the men, Demetrios recognized the two instructors as Marcus and his partner, Anthony.

Demetrios fell on his knees before Marcus in a deep bow of respect. "Excuse me. May I have a word with you?"

Marcus turned to Anthony and ordered him to continue with the exercise. To Demetrios, who rose to his feet, he asked, "Can I be of service?"

"Yes, you can," replied Demetrios. "Governor Pilate requests your presence at his palace. I am Demetrios, the personal servant of the governor. He directed me to this location. He assumed, and he was right, that you would be here with your partner, Anthony, practicing battle tactics. He has a bit of a dilemma, and he needs your expertise. I have orders to advise you that Pilate himself will explain the situation."

Marcus turned to Anthony once again and said, "Let's go. The lesson is over. Tell the men we will let them know when we will meet again." Gesturing toward Demetrios, Marcus said, "Pontius Pilate's servant informs me that Pilate wishes to see us immediately at his estate. Apparently he has an urgent matter. We don't want to keep him waiting."

As they rode their horses toward the governor's estate, Marcus asked his young partner, "How's your son? I heard he's been sick."

Sadness was an unfamiliar emotion to Anthony, who was usually ebullient and enthusiastic, and he wore the somber mood of the serious turn of the discussion like an ill-fitting cloak.

After a moment he responded impatiently. "Not so good. I have had the best doctors examine him, but he still constantly coughs and complains that his body aches. The doctors don't know what ails him." Anthony hesitated. Glancing at Marcus from the corner of his eye, he continued, "My wife is beside herself. Nothing is more important than his health. We have a Jewish servant girl who has taken a great interest in him. I've noticed when she thinks no one is looking she prays to her god for our son. That I appreciate. We can use the help of the gods."

Deliberately changing the subject, Marcus asked, "Does your wife still make boiled ostrich like she used to?"

Anthony's smile returned. He said, "You can see for yourself. She invites you to dinner, and she won't accept no for an answer."

Several minutes passed in silence, and Anthony hoped his senior partner would overlook his boldness.

At the palace entrance, Marcus frowned at the figure on the terrace. "Is that Pilate? My eyesight is not what it once was."

Anthony stared in the same direction. "Yes, it's him."

Nodding, Marcus said, "I don't want to get on the wrong side of your wife. I thank her for the invitation. I haven't had a home-cooked meal for many months. We'll talk about when we will share that meal after we find out what is going on here now."

Inside the palace, Marcus grabbed Anthony by the shoulders and spun him so their eyes would meet. "Anthony, we must be careful what we say and how we say it. Pilate may come off civilized, but he can be like a mad dog if he doesn't get what he wants. He is as treacherous as they come. He believes there is a conspiracy behind every door. I want you to say nothing. Let me do the talking. You got that?"

"But what—"

"Don't question me!" Marcus barked.

Abashed, Anthony had to run to keep pace with the furious steps of his partner as he marched toward the terrace and Pilate.

• • •

Marcus bowed his head and extended his hand in greeting to the governor.

"Your Highness, it is a privilege to be of service. We came as soon as we were told of your request. What can we do for you?"

With his hands clasped behind his back, walking from one palace window to another, Pilate responded, "You can kill every Jewish priest in Judea, that's what you can do for me. *Every one!* They are nothing but a nuisance, constantly complaining, never satisfied, a thorn in my side. They don't serve their people; they serve themselves. How I let myself get caught in the middle of their religious squabbling I will never know."

Coming to stand before the two men, Pilate asked them, "Did you hear what happened in Jerusalem these last few days?"

"I'm not sure what you mean," Marcus answered. "I heard there were several crucifixions, but that's not news, is it?"

Pilate shook his head, slammed his fist on his nearby writing table, and shouted, "You know it amazes me that my wife for the first time in her miserable life here gave me good advice, and I didn't take it! How did she know this event would cause me problems? A dream, she says." Pilate shook his head again, mystified.

Confused, Marcus cleared his throat and ventured a question. "Your Highness, I don't understand. What are you saying?"

Sitting down on his Seat of Judgment, Pilate heaved a deep sigh. "I shall have to start from the beginning. For a while…a couple of years…the temple priests have been complaining about one of their own kind, a Jew named Jesus. According to them he is another self proclaimed messiah. You know this occurs on a regular basis in that community?"

At the nodding of the two men, Pilate continued, "I cannot concern myself with their internal disputes, but they began insisting that this Jesus was arousing the people and ordering them not to pay their taxes. They also alleged that this Jesus promoted himself as king. Ridiculous, I know. It was evident to me that the priests were only concerned with their agenda, keeping their power and control over the people. My concern was not the priests but the possibility of one of Herod's cohorts finding out that I did nothing to deal with these allegations. The tetrarchs like to flaunt their own connections with Rome."

Pilate muttered this last with venom. "In any event, on the morning of their preparation day, following their Passover feast, the priests and temple elders came to me, making these claims about Jesus. They had him in custody. He was beaten. Bound and bleeding. It was pathetic." Pilate turned his back to the men at the violence of the recollection.

Marcus and Anthony exchanged frowns. Brutality was commonplace throughout the empire. It was a necessary means for keeping the mob under control. Pilate's reputation for savagery was legendary. The men were puzzled and wondered about this Jesus.

"The High Priest was Caiaphas," Pilate went on. "He was accompanied by a few others. They demanded Roman justice." Pilate allowed himself an ironic smile.

"I asked this Jesus if he heard their accusations. He had to have heard, but he seemed disinterested in what was happening! I thought that he may not have understood the seriousness of the charges, perhaps he was simpleminded," Pilate said, with a wave of his hand. "Still, he did not respond. He did not answer with regard to even one single charge. I was quite amazed."

Pilate rose and walked to the sideboard, where he poured himself a glass of water. Marcus could see the beads of sweat breaking out across the governor's forehead and along his upper lip. He did not dare to risk another look at Anthony, and again he marveled at this man Jesus' effect on the Roman procurator.

Pilate dabbed at the moisture collecting on his face with a towel and then continued with the story. "He was so calm it was disconcerting. You would think that he would make a defense for himself. Why didn't he defend himself... ? I finally asked him, are you the king of the Jews?"

Pilate was silent so long that Marcus finally spoke. Clearing his throat, he said, "Governor?"

Pilate met Marcus's eyes and went on as though nothing had happened. "He answered me. He said it is as you say." Regaining his rage, Pilate clasped his hands behind his back and roared, "Why in the name of the gods would he answer like that? He could have responded no, and that would have been the end of their case! And life would have been made much easier for me." Pilate sighed and said, "Well, I found no guilt in him. It was clear that he committed no crime, nothing deserving of death. So I told the Jewish jackals in their long black robes that I found no guilt in this man, but they kept insisting he had been teaching sedition, beginning in Galilee. When I heard them say Galilee, I asked if the man was a Galilean. That placed him in Herod's jurisdiction. Herod would have to adjudicate the accusation. I sent him to Herod."

Unable to restrain himself, Anthony shifted his weight on his feet. Marcus stiffened. He hoped the governor would not notice the youth's impatience. When the governor went on unperturbed, Marcus found himself suddenly thankful for Pilate's strange preoccupation with the Jewish lunatic.

"That pompous pig Herod sent him back. Herod was not amused by Jesus' lack of magical powers."

At this, Marcus and Anthony could not contain their confusion, and Pilate chuckled at their bewilderment. "Apparently Herod asked Jesus to perform magic tricks in exchange for his release. There has been talk of *miracles*. But Jesus did not perform for Herod. He ended up in my courtyard once again."

Pilate again returned to the sideboard. This time, however, he filled the glass with wine, emptying the glass before continuing. "I think under other circumstances I would have enjoyed the man's company."

Pilate poured himself more wine and walked to the bank of windows. "We began to debate the concept of truth. In fact, we went back and forth about it. What is truth, what truth is." Turning to face the men, Pilate said, "I'll tell you, he was a very different kind of person. And that was a very different kind of night."

Pausing for a moment Pilate continued, "Marcus, do you believe that a person can see into the future?" Perplexed by the conversation and mention of miracles and magic tricks, Marcus was unsure how to respond. He decided to answer truthfully.

"No."

Pilate nodded. It had been the answer he expected from a Roman soldier. It would have been the answer he himself would have given a few days ago. Now, he was feeling unsettled and no longer certain of anything he once believed.

"My wife sent one of our servants to me while I was on the Judgment Seat dealing with the fate of Jesus. She had given the servant a bizarre message. She had had a dream or vision." Pilate waved the hand that held the glass of wine. "She said, 'Have nothing to do with this righteous man.' I didn't pay heed to her words, Marcus. I was already going to free him. I had examined him and found him not guilty. Herod, the Jew, sent him back without finding him guilty either."

Pilate's voice rose with passion and indignation. "I told the Jews I would punish him and release him, but that wasn't good enough for them, the blood-thirsty dogs. It appeared that I was going to have an uprising. But you know I have this custom of releasing a prisoner chosen by the crowd for their Passover. I am too merciful." Pilate began to pace the room. "Naturally, I thought they would choose Jesus. He was no murderer. He had healed them! So the stories go. But they chose to free Barabbas."

Pilate once again came to stand before the men. "They sentenced Jesus to die. '*Crucify him*!' they shouted, *Crucify him!* The crowds did it. The Jews did it. Not I."

Pilate returned to his writing table and collapsed in the chair. "I literally washed my hands of him. The blood of this man is on them. I had him scourged. He was crucified on the hill. I was surprised when the guards told me he was dead; he died quickly. But then again, he had suffered much blood loss. When Joseph of Arimethea, a member of the Jewish council, requested the body for burial, I was glad to be relieved of the foul mess. It was over, or so I thought."

Pilate looked grim. "Those infernal priests returned to request an audience with me. They were concerned that Jesus' disciples would return and steal the body from the tomb. Among his many great feats, this Jesus promised that he would rise from the dead, so they told me. Because he made that assertion the priests were concerned that his followers would return to the tomb, steal the body, and then propagate the rumor that he arose from the dead." Pilate could not keep the sarcasm from his voice. "They wanted a guard posted at the tomb. That made sense to me, so I dispatched a contingent to accompany their own temple guards with orders for securing and sealing the tomb. I must tell you I would have rather impaled those treacherous priests for all the trouble they caused me, but I had to consider the possibility that they may be right and things would get worse."

"Your Highness, I still don't understand what the problem is," Marcus said.

Furious, Pilate yelled, "My problem…my problem… my problem is he is *missing*!" The body is gone. Disappeared. Vanished without a trace. This fiasco will cause me great embarrassment, not to mention bring into question my ability to rule. This demonstrates a lack of discipline in our ranks. This incident could ignite unrest in the region. We don't need this kind of publicity getting back to Rome."

Rising from his chair, Pilate addressed the men, and Marcus could tell they were finally receiving their orders.

"I need you and Anthony to investigate this treasonous act against Roman authority. You will retrieve the body, apprehend the thieves, and I will make an example out of them. When I am through with them, it will be quite a show—worthy of the Coliseum. However, it is important you be as discreet as possible. This must be kept secret. You can begin your investigation at the burial place selected by Joseph of Arimathea. It is located near the crucifixion site."

Standing at attention, Marcus responded, "Your Highness, I am aware of the burial sites. We will proceed to the crime scene without delay. This should be a short investigation. The most probable explanation is that his followers removed the body. We will know soon enough."

Marcus raised his fist to his heart and forward toward Pilate, turning his head toward Anthony and quickly back to Pilate.

"Your Highness, do you have any intelligence information on his disciples? If you do, I would like a list of those Jews who are followers of this Jesus. Their names, addresses, and places that they gather would be most helpful. We will begin a full investigation as to their whereabouts on that night and on the days since. Also, do you know where I can find the guards who secured and guarded the tomb?"

"Yes, Demetrios will provide you with the information you have requested. The guards who were assigned to the crucifixion and security of the tomb are stationed at the garrison. Marcus, take this letter and seal. This gives you the power and authority of my position to complete your investigation. No one has the power or authority to interfere with your investigation without severe punishment from Rome. Whatever you request from the Roman citizens, including soldiers of a higher rank, they must comply or face my wrath." Pilate peered intently into the face of Marcus. "Do you understand the extent of your power?"

"Yes, sir, I do," Marcus responded, "and I will use it to bring glory to you and Rome. We will proceed to the tomb to begin an initial investigation."

• • •

Demetrious provided limited information concerning some of Jesus' followers, but it was enough to start an investigation. The two men held their counsel as they saddled their horses and headed in the direction of the burial ground. After a while, Anthony turned to Marcus and said, "He looked as angry as a female lion whose cubs are missing. What do you think he's going to do to those thieves when we apprehend them?"

Shaking his head, Marcus replied, "I'm more concerned with what he will do to us if we don't solve this quickly. You must remember he is the Roman governor of Palestine. That didn't happen overnight or because he is lucky. He knows how to get things done and eliminate threats. And his wrath, as he said, will fall on anyone, including us."

"You know it seems suspicious that this body went missing when there were Roman guards stationed at the site for just that purpose," Anthony said.

Wrinkling his brow, Marcus concurred. "The thought had occurred to me, as well. How would these rebels be able to remove the body with guards stationed outside the tomb?"

The hill where the crucifixion had taken place was called Golgotha—the skull, for its macabre shape. Just north of the hill was the garden, the burial ground of the Jews. Marcus and Anthony had learned that Jesus was buried in a tomb that had been carved in the rock for Joseph of Arimathea, a rich man. Joseph had given his own sepulcher for use by the lunatic, as Marcus thought of him.

A row of date palms formed a border to the garden, which was filled with an abundance of plants and flowers. The aroma sweetened the air, and the men found themselves lifting their noses to take in the welcome scents, a pleasant change from the odor of horse flesh and their own perspiring bodies in need of baths.

"Lovely," Anthony murmured. Embarrassed to have spoken aloud, he said, "All right, all right, I just was making an observation."

Smiling, Marcus said, "Observe the scene, Anthony. That's what we're here for. I want you to document all our observations. Furthermore, you will prioritize the list of the individuals we have to interrogate. We'll know better in what direction to proceed after we analyze the scene. Here it is. Let's go in."

Scene of the Crime

Anthony hesitated at the entrance of the tomb. Entering used tombs, disturbing the dead, was not customarily done. This tomb, particularly, had been prepared by the stone mason to remain sealed. He felt the chill of being watched by the gods and could not refrain from glancing over his shoulder. There was no one there; not even an animal moved about in the midday heat. Still, Anthony felt the hairs rise from his neck. What had happened here that he should feel such white-hot energy in the air?

The tomb of a rich man, the stone mason's work was very fine. The stone used to seal the tomb weighed two tons. The Roman seal, placed over the stone, had been broken. Anthony wondered, *Who would dare to risk death for this crime*?

From within the tomb, Marcus said, "That's unusual."

"Everything about this crime scene is unusual," said Anthony, entering the darkened crypt.

Marcus pointed. There, on the stone slab where the body had lain, were linen cloths. "Empty grave clothes. Material evidence."

The cloths gave no evidence of a struggle. They were not scattered or tossed, not even twisted. It appeared as though the body had simply moved through the cloths. This discovery was so odd that the men were silent while they absorbed the implications.

Finally, Anthony stated, "Obviously, someone removed the body. But who would remove the wrappings from the body? And why?"

Putting his finger to his lips, Marcus whispered, "Calm down, Anthony. Let's take it slow and methodically. There could be several explanations, and we will come up with the right one."

Set aside from the linens was a neatly folded piece of material, used by the Jews as a facial covering. "Why would the thieves take the time to fold the face cloth?" Anthony wanted to know.

"I am sure there is a logical explanation. Before we determine that the wrappings were removed from the body, let's determine that there was in fact a dead body in these wrappings."

"Of course there was a body. Our guards were here when the body was placed in the tomb and the entrance rock secured it," said Anthony.

"I don't mean that. The body was here, but was he dead? If he were alive he would have to remove the wrappings in order to make his escape," Marcus barked. "There are several possibilities regarding a missing corpse, and the first possibility is that there never was a dead body in this tomb."

"Pilate said—"

"Think, Anthony! We have established nothing at this point. I know what Pilate said; however, we must confirm everything that has been reported, and that takes time. So be quiet while I continue with some possible theories.

One, there never was a dead body in this tomb. Two, there was a body in this tomb, and a person or persons removed it. Three, there was a body in this tomb, but he was not dead, and he removed himself. Four, there was a live body in this tomb, and with the help of co-conspirators he escaped."

Anthony waited as instructed for Marcus to collect his thoughts.

"Most disturbing, Anthony, is that we must consider the possibility of a conspiracy with our own guards. I mean, how could anyone break the Roman seal and move that massive stone without alerting a single one of the guards? Units of two or more men were here all night." Shaking his head, Marcus added, "Of course, that seems outrageous. Our soldiers despise these Jews as much as they despise us, but I suppose every man has his price. The right price can buy anything—cooperation of any kind from anyone."

Grinning, Anthony said, "Isn't there a sixth possibility? And I find it peculiar that you have not mentioned it since you're an expert in the Hebrew studies."

Marcus grunted, "What is that, Anthony?"

"That he rose from the dead? Isn't that one of the possibilities, the dead man rising to life?"

With a sardonic lift of his eyebrows, Marcus replied, "I won't even waste my breath in answering that question. Perhaps I should send for another investigator. I need one who is thinking clearly. If you want to entertain the notion of ghosts, we will never get to the bottom of this."

Marcus walked out of the tomb, and Anthony followed close behind. The sunlight was blinding after the dimness of the tomb. Anthony sucked air into his lungs and realized he had been barely breathing in the tomb, refusing to breathe in particles of dust that may have been particles of decay. *Death is an unnatural state for man*, he thought. *It is as foreign to us as fire is to our skin.*

The men began canvassing the perimeter of the area for evidence of what had occurred. Marcus had already noted that the ground within the tomb revealed the boot print of a Roman guard. It appeared only one had entered a few paces and then exited. There were three, possibly four, sets of sandals that approached the stone slab and then retreated. None of the sets had the appearance of bearing the heavy weight of a dead human body, even those sandal prints that left the slab. There were no prints of bare feet.

As he searched the outside area, Anthony found it unimaginable that his fellow soldiers would have failed in this task. The Roman soldiers were strictly disciplined fighting men. Could they have fallen asleep, risking torture, humiliation, and death? Had they been overpowered? Anthony surmised that it would have taken a legion of men to overcome these soldiers of Rome, whose motto was, "Come home with your shield or on it."

"What are you doing?" Marcus asked, as he observed Anthony attempting to move the entrance rock.

"Attempting to establish how many suspects it would take to move this thing." Embarrassed by the question, Anthony shrugged his shoulders sheepishly. "I was just seeing if I was strong enough to move it myself. Guess not."

Anthony turned his attention back to the garden area, which was perfectly peaceful and gave no evidence of a struggle. Nor could Anthony find any spaces of flattened grass or smoothed-out sand that would have indicated a sleeping site. He observed identifiable prints of civilian sandals that crossed over the boot prints of the guards, which meant that the civilians had approached after the guards left their position. It also appeared that some of the civilians had run up to the tomb, walked in, and left the scene walking. It was evident by the distance between the boot prints of the guards that they ran or at least hurried from the tomb.

Anthony relayed this information to Marcus. Together they scoured the area for further clues, refusing to accept what appeared to be a clean scene. After spending several hours at the scene, they heard a sudden shout in the distance. The men found themselves watching an approaching cloud of dust, at the center of which would be a man on a horse—one of Pilate's personal bodyguards, sent to order them back to the palace for new information.

Making their way out of the garden, Anthony stared longingly at the pomegranates and fig trees. He felt the rush of saliva in his mouth. It had been a long time since he had eaten.

"Will you dine with us tonight?" he asked Marcus.

Marcus smiled. "That would be welcomed, my friend. Let us see about this new information, and then we will call an end to the day. I look forward to visiting with your family."

When they arrived at the palace they were met by Demetrios, who escorted them to Pilate's private chambers in the north wing of the palace. Ushered inside the chambers, Marcus and Anthony marveled at the rich display of wealth and power. They had heard rumors of Pilate's majestic quarters, but the common soldier was never invited here.

The walls gleamed white marble with blue onyx running across the bottom trim. The paintings on the wall were framed in pure gold. Pilate was sitting in a chair that rivaled any royal throne, the deeply padded backrest rising two feet above the head of the governor. Pilate rested his head on his hand, and he appeared to be meditating, unaware of the presence of the men.

Marcus cleared his throat, clicked his heels, and spoke in a voice just above a whisper. "Your Highness, you requested we return? How can we be of service?"

Through tight lips Pilate responded, "It is being reported by the Jewish elders that the rebels came by night and stole the body while the guards were sleeping. Our *guards*! Our Roman soldiers! This is preposterous!" Pilate fixed his tiny eyes on Marcus. "But I wasn't there. You were. Is it possible they fell asleep and did not hear people approaching?"

Marcus said, "Your Highness, I am not prepared to make a report yet. Our investigation is far from complete."

"The seriousness of these allegations warrants an immediate response. The guards' behavior is suspect at best. Thieves could not have moved the rock at the entranceway without making plenty of noise," said Pilate, and again he looked at Marcus. "Dereliction in their duty is punishable by death. How in the name of the gods does a group of soldiers fall asleep while such a crime takes place only steps away from them? There has to be another explanation."

Summoning Demetrios from where he stood in the shadows by the doorway, Pilate ordered the servant to proceed to the Jewish quarter, find the chief priest, and bring him to the palace.

"If he is unwilling, tell him he will be arrested. That should put fire to his feet. I want him here now. I'll get to the bottom of this one way or another. I believe that he also had his temple guards stationed at the tomb. If that is the case, bring them all along, as well."

"Your Highness, Anthony and I will proceed to the garrison. We will make inquiries and interview the captain and his men. We will be very discreet." Marcus bowed his head. "Please allow us to contact the priest and his guards. As we gather the facts, we will be able to detect the lies."

Pilate pondered Marcus's suggestion. Then he asked, "What has your investigation uncovered thus far?"

Marcus grimaced. He hated preemptory conclusions, and the crime scene had revealed too little information. But he could not refuse Pilate's direct question.

"Sir, the tomb disclosed nothing of significant value in determining who may have perpetrated this crime or how. There were suspicious signs. The rock that had sealed the tomb was moved much farther away than was required to gain entry. That was odd. The rock itself weighs at least two tons easily and would have required several men to move it. Furthermore, like most sepulchers, the entrance has a deep groove cut out in the ground, so when the rock is rolled to its resting place it locks itself in the groove at the bottom making it very difficult to remove the rock once it's in place. Additionally, there was the Roman seal, which was broken. There appeared to be a variety of footprints leading to and away from the tomb. Some of the prints appeared to be civilian; others were the boot prints of Roman or temple guards. It appears that three, maybe four people actually entered the tomb. It's difficult to say with certainty because some prints overlapped others, and that made them indistinguishable."

"That's it? You were there all day, and that's all the information you gathered? I could have sent anyone to gather that kind of information. What good is that to me? I need results *now*!"

Angered by Pilate's criticism, Marcus bellowed, "*No, that is not all!* There are more details to explain."

Pilate's snake-like eyes grew paler. He spoke quietly. "I realize that you have connections in Rome. That means nothing to me. If you ever display that insubordinate attitude again I'll have you charged, jailed, and impaled. Do you understand me?"

"I apologize for my arrogant and rude behavior," Marcus answered the governor. "There is no excuse. It will not happen again."

Pilate waited several seconds before asking Marcus to continue. Moderating his voice to a pitch without emotion, Marcus said, "Outside the tomb there was no sign or indication of a struggle. No sign or indication of a disturbance from a large crowd or multitude." Nervously, Marcus drew in a deep breath and went on. "Inside the tomb was quite peculiar. When we entered the tomb there was some *material evidence*. The grave cloths were still there. They lay in the same position that the body would have been in had the body been there. In other words they were not unwound and left in a pile. It looked as if the body went *through* the wrappings, as if they weren't there."

Pilate frowned and worked his mouth, at a loss for words.

"Yes, sir, it's a bit of a mystery. It makes no sense to us either."

"Yes, yes. There are several problems. Do you have any explanations or theories?"

"We do not as of yet. I would like to interrogate those guards who were assigned to security as soon as possible. However, we're going to have to start from the beginning. We need to establish for a fact that this Jesus actually died on the cross. There's much we have to do. We will make a list of all persons we wish to interview. We will organize a plan of action and systematically uncover all the facts to this case."

"Do you think there was some type of conspiracy between the Jewish rebels and my guards?" Pilate asked. Realizing that Marcus had provided as much knowledge as he could, Pilate dismissed his own question. "You must go on with your investigation. Just keep me informed."

• • •

Night had fallen while they were in the palace, and the men welcomed the relief of the cool, moist air. The hint of dampness touched their faces like a lingering kiss. The horses carefully picked their way among the rock-strewn road. Marcus glanced sideways at the youth beside him and wondered if he should bring up his own error in allowing his temper to flare before the governor. He decided to let the matter stand as it was; it would be a lesson to the young man, who was often too impulsive himself.

Instead, he let his thoughts turn to tomorrow and his plans for the investigation. To Anthony he said, "I need to establish for myself that this Jesus was dead when he was removed from the cross."

Interviews at the Garrison

Anthony's entire household lay sleeping, so late was the hour when they finally made their way to the modest home. Not willing to disturb his wife, Anthony gathered bread and honeycomb, beans and lentils, along with a decanter of water and a decanter of wine. The men reclined at the table and enjoyed the food in silence.

Afterward, Anthony led Marcus to a guest bedroom at the rear of the house. "Make yourself comfortable. Get some rest. We'll talk in the morning."

Brilliant yellow sunlight poured like melted butter into Marcus's room through the narrow window above the bed on which he lay. He stretched his limbs luxuriously and yawned widely before slitting his eyes open against the sun. He had slept so restfully. Insomnia had come to be his permanent nighttime companion, and his surprise at sleeping peacefully through the night was matched by his appreciation of it.

With a sudden start, though, Marcus remembered the pressing tasks ahead; and he was dismayed to see how advanced the sun was already. Hurriedly he dressed.

As Marcus exited the room, he met Anthony coming to summon him for breakfast.

Anthony smiled. "Did you sleep well?"

"Look how high the sun is," Marcus replied brusquely. "We have much to do. I feel we will have better luck after we interview the soldiers that witnessed these events. Let's ride to the garrison and get to work."

"Wait a minute." Anthony placed a restraining hand on Marcus' shoulder. "You have not greeted my wife and son. She has been up for hours preparing the morning meal."

"You are right. My mind is on our mission. It would be a privilege and an honor to eat with your family." Anthony clapped Marcus on the back. "Come. The food is waiting."

As Marcus fit his solid, muscle-bound frame alongside the low table, he raked his fingers through his blue-black hair, sweeping it back from his face in an attempt to brush and smooth his hair before Anthony's wife, Madelyn, would see him. Marcus was a very handsome man, completely unaware of his striking good looks, but he did know that women appreciated good hygiene and cleanliness.

When Madelyn entered the room, Marcus rose to greet her. His partner's wife was a beautiful woman, with luminous dark eyes and a mass of black curls that tumbled to the small of her back. Dressed simply and chastely, Madelyn's flowing gown could not hide the generous curves of her figure, her ample breasts, the tiny waist, her rounded bottom.

Madelyn greeted Marcus with a sisterly hug. "I hear that you are taking good care of my husband," she said, and added with a conspiratorial smile, "I know that he is a handful at times."

"That he is," Marcus nodded, quickly adding, "He is an honorable man."

As Marcus was speaking, Anthony's young son rushed into the room and threw himself into his father's arms. "Father, I've missed you! What have you been doing? Did you bring me a present? Who is your friend?"

"Who—"

Anthony held up his hand. "Easy, Son, one question at a time. As you can see, Marcus, this is my son, Tiberius. Tiberius, shake hands with Marcus."

Marcus shook the boy's hand. "What a handsome boy you are. Thank the gods you look like your mother. How old are you, Tiberius?"

"I am nine years and two months. And I can use a sword. After we eat, would you like to see?"

"Yes, of course." Marcus could see that Tiberius, his mother's son with Madelyn's eyes and dark curly hair, was ill. His face appeared pale and ashen. But the boy was clearly a fighter, and that was good.

On the table were bowls of freshly-picked fruit, and Madelyn added loaves of hot, steaming bread and boiled eggs. After serving the men, she joined them. Marcus noted that Madelyn never inquired as to what the men were up to; she only asked how things were going. He appreciated her calm and her reticence. He could also see that she was gentle and kind, and he hoped that his friend Anthony understood how rich he was.

As soon as they were done eating, the men went outside so Tiberius could demonstrate his ability with the sword. Marcus was glad to see that the boy was quite good. Then Marcus excused himself to saddle the horses, telling Anthony to say his good-byes.

• • •

As he entered the stable, Marcus saw a young Jewish maiden tending the horses. He greeted her and said, "I am Marcus, a friend of Anthony."

Staring at the ground, she responded, "I am Ruth, a servant of Master Anthony."

In spite of his haste to be off, Marcus found himself drawn to the girl. "How long have you served this house, Ruth?" he asked.

"For several years my sister and I have been cared for by Master Anthony. We have come to love him and his family," and Ruth's eyes filled with tears.

"What is the trouble? Something has saddened you. What is it?"

"My master's son is very sick. We have had the best physicians examine him, and yet the sickness still persists. I am afraid for him. We pray day and night that our God will heal him."

"*God!*" Marcus could not contain his agitation. "No, what we need is to locate the best doctors. Even if I must go to Rome I will make inquires. I have some old connections. As soon as time permits I will attempt to make contact with them." Softening his voice, he added, "I thank you for that information. I will keep it confidential."

"I am ready," shouted Anthony from outside the stable, "Let's go!"

As they made their way toward the garrison, Marcus said, "You have an admirable family. You should be very proud."

Almost involuntarily, Anthony felt his chest swell. "Thank you. That means a lot coming from you."

As they continued on, Marcus was debating whether he should ask Anthony about Ruth. Marcus had encountered opportunities to start new relationships but had found no one of interest since his wife had passed. But Ruth intrigued him.

"Ruth seems to be a very loyal servant," said Marcus.

Anthony perceived Marcus's interest. "What makes you say that?"

"Never mind. I'm not going to play your game, Anthony."

"I'm only teasing. Yes, she is a loyal and faithful servant. In reality she is a very important part of my family. She is both strong and compassionate. And I think you two would—"

Marcus pointed. "Look for the captain of the garrison. The captain should be able to direct us to the soldiers we are looking for. They are probably under his command."

As they continued their approach Anthony said, "Is that him? That can't be him."

They both stared at the baffling sight of a large, muscular man in full battle gear with what appeared to be women's make-up on his face.

"That can't be the uniform of the day," Anthony remarked, and the two men laughed.

Marcus and Anthony got off their horses and were met at the entrance of the garrison by the man, who merely nodded when Marcus inquired if he were the captain.

"We have been ordered by Pilate to interview the soldiers that were assigned to the crucifixion detail last week. We have his signet to confirm our authority. We're wondering if you could direct us to them."

As Marcus was speaking, the captain abruptly interrupted. "What's this all about? I've received no orders or directives from the governor in reference to your orders. What exactly are you attempting to uncover?" Suddenly, as if noticing Marcus for the first time, the captain said, "You look familiar. Oh yes, now I remember. Aren't you the centurion that married some Jew girl—

Marcus lunged at the captain and ruthlessly beat him to the ground. Anthony grabbed Marcus before he killed the man.

"Easy, partner...calm down."

Turning to the captain, who was coughing, spitting blood, and holding his neck, Anthony continued, "We are here to interview the soldiers who were detailed to the crucifixion that occurred last Friday. If you want to act like an arrogant idiot, I'll let him beat you to a pulp."

Blood seeped from the captain's broken nose and trickled out of the corners of his mangled mouth.

Reluctantly, he pointed to the Praetorium, which is the proper name for the garrison. Still choking and coughing he mumbled, "They're inside, probably still sleeping."

His face was beginning to swell and talking was becoming more difficult, but the captain went on through clenched jaws. "This Praetorian is part of Herod's palace. He has the authority here. I answer to Herod. And he will be informed of your insolence. I outrank you, and you had no business raising your hands to me. You haven't heard the last of this, Centurion; Herod will be informed of your insubordination. I will see you jailed for this crime."

Marcus ignored the captain, who was now badly in need of medical attention, and entered the garrison.

Once inside, Anthony exclaimed, "What in the name of the gods were you trying to prove? The captain was just making a statement. Your wife was a Jew, wasn't she? So what's the big deal? Why would that bother you? Why would you attack him like that?"

Keeping his eyes fixed forward, Marcus said, "I'm not interested in talking about it now. Let's just get this job done."

• • •

The rooms of the garrison were extremely large in size. Hundreds of soldiers could comfortably stay in there. There were several cooking areas and dozens of servants. There were stockpiles of all types of weapons.

"Get someone's attention," Marcus directed the younger man.

Anthony shouted to a soldier standing at the back entrance, "Can we talk to you a minute?"

The soldier approached and asked, "What can I do for you?"

"We're looking for the soldiers that were detailed to the crucifixion scene last Friday. Do you know where we can find them?"

The soldier replied, "Most of the cohorts were called out early this morning, about four o'clock. Apparently there's a minor rebellion in Joppa, northeast of here, by the great sea. They were ordered to that scene to squash it. However, I was detailed to that crucifixion with other soldiers from my squad. They're somewhere around town. I couldn't tell you where. If you hang around I'm sure they'll be back before nightfall."

Anthony responded, "Appreciate the information. My name is Anthony, and this is Marcus."

The men shook hands, and the soldier said, "I'm Julius."

"Governor Pontius Pilate assigned us to investigate the crucifixion that occurred last Friday at Golgotha," Marcus explained. "We are specifically interested in the chronology of the events."

Looking confused, Julius inquired, "What does that mean? We execute several, even dozens of criminals a week. Which one are you interested in? And why are you interested?"

"There was more than one execution?" asked Anthony.

"Yes," said Julius. "Like I said, we execute many criminals in the course of a week. Now, if you're talking about the executions at Golgotha, there were three males executed there that day."

Enthusiastically Anthony responded, "We are interested in the Jew named Jesus."

Smiling and shaking his head, Julius said, "How did I know you were going to say that?"

"What do you mean?"

Julius continued, "In all the years that I've been assigned to this duty I've never witnessed a criminal being crucified that acted like him… "

"I don't mean to cut you off, but would you explain to us exactly what you witnessed from beginning to end?"

"Yes, sure," Julius answered. "But what are you looking for? I mean, we crucified him, he died, and he was removed from the cross and taken to a grave site. Is there some type of allegation against me or my men concerning our handling of the event?"

"No allegations," said Anthony. "But we can't get into all the details. It's a need-to-know investigation ordered by the governor. He was very emphatic about that. The details of this investigation are to be kept secret."

Looking perplexed and concerned, Julius said, "What do you want to know?"

"We need to know everything you witnessed from the moment you took charge of him."

Julius nodded. "My squad was summoned to the Praetorium, the garrison under Pilate's authority, which as you know is also where Pilate's official residence is located. When we arrived Pilate was sitting on the Judgment Seat at a place called the Pavement.

There were numerous soldiers at the scene. I recognized some. Most are specifically assigned to the protection of Pilate. The others were from my garrison and under the authority of Herod.

"A mob had crowded into that area. They were agitated, violent, and rowdy. I observed standing in front of Pilate this prisoner. It appeared to me that his presence was the cause of the agitated crowd. Later, I was informed that he was in fact the reason for the angry crowd. I was also informed that he was a Jew, and his name was Jesus.

One of the soldiers at the scene stated that this Jesus had just returned from Herod's palace and was being sentenced to death for treasonous statements against the empire. It appeared that he had already received some of the sentence because he was physically beaten.

"Some of the soldiers were mocking him. Apparently he called himself the king of the Jews, so the guards made a crown for the king of the Jews, made out of palm leaves.

You know they have sharp spines that can cut you open like a razor, and they had shoved it onto his head.

"They scourged him with a whip of leather thongs—the whip with small pieces of metal tied to the thongs. His whole body from his head to his ankles was a bloody mess.

My squad and I took charge of him, and we led him away to Golgotha. Because he was beaten so badly we forced a citizen into service. We ordered this man to assist King Jesus with his cross. He attempted to carry it himself, but he fell under many times. When we arrived at Golgotha we set things up and nailed him to the cross. Subsequently he died, and in accordance with Pilate's orders we released the corpse to some Jews who requested it."

"Did your men follow procedure when they crucified him, and if so explain to me exactly what they did?"

Julius answered, "Of course, we know of no other way. We never cut corners. As you know, it's our most severe form of execution, so it's reserved for slaves and criminals. It involves attaching the prisoner with nails through the wrists to a crossbeam attached to a vertical stake. Sometimes blocks or pins are put on the stake to give the prisoner some support as he hangs suspended from the crossbeam. At times the feet are also nailed to the vertical stake. As the prisoner hangs dangling by the arms, the blood can no longer circulate to his vital organs. Only by supporting himself on the block or pin could the prisoner gain relief. Gradually exhaustion sets in, and death follows, although usually not for several days. If the prisoner had been severely beaten, he would not live that long. Sometimes for one reason or another we are ordered to hasten death. When that's the case, my guards break the prisoner's legs with a heavy hammer or club. The effect of breaking their legs causes them to no longer be able to support their body. They suffocate."

"Did you witness your men performing their assignment?" asked Anthony.

Julius shook his head. "No, not exactly. I was summoned by one of my soldiers to assist them further down the road. There was a disruptive group hurling rocks at the soldiers who were lining the road leading to Golgotha. So I left orders for them to complete their assignments. I left my post and preceded to the location were the disturbance was taking place. When I returned the dead body was being released to several Jews."

Anthony asked, "Did you in fact see this Jesus die on the cross?"

Julius paused, "No. I assumed he was dead. What else could he be?"

"Did your soldiers break his legs?"

Nervously Julius responded, "I assumed they did, but I'm not certain. You will have to ask them. Am I in trouble? Look, I've handled dozens of crucifixions. We always follow procedure. You have to believe me. I have never taken a prisoner off a cross until it has been positively established he was dead. You must believe me."

Empathizing, Anthony responded, "We are attempting to establish the facts concerning the crucifixion and death of this Jesus. If there's nothing more you can add, we would like to interview the rest of your squad right away."

"There are several of them around. Give me a few minutes, and I'll round them up. If you like you can use the officers' quarters for your interviews."

"Thanks, soldier," said Marcus, "we will take you up on that."

As Julius left to find his fellow squad members and Marcus and Anthony made their way to the officers' quarters, the two men discussed their strategy. Believing that the soldiers would be forthright concerning their involvement and observation, the men decided that there would be no need for rough tactics. However, they agreed that the best approach would be to separate them, interviewing the soldiers in small groups of two or three at a time. It all seemed cut and dry.

After about ten minutes of discussion, Julius arrived accompanied by six soldiers.

"Here they are. They can answer all your questions. I explained to them that you are investigating the crucifixions of those criminals last Friday. They will be more than happy to assist you in any way they can. Marcus, Anthony, this is Latinius, Nemonius, Petilluis, Victor, Varius, and Felix." The men shook hands all around. "They were all involved in one aspect or another of the final executions. If you don't mind, I have some unfinished business I have to attend to. I will return shortly."

"Julius, we appreciate your cooperation," said Marcus. Turning his attention to the six soldiers he requested, "We would like to first interview the guys that actually nailed the one called Jesus to the cross. Then we'll interview the rest accordingly. So then, who would that be?"

"That would be us," Latinius and Nemonius responded in unison. "We are expert executioners," said Latinius, laughing. "We've been doing this for several years now. And it's not as easy as it looks."

"I'm sure it's not," Anthony said abruptly. Looking at the other four soldiers Anthony ordered them to wait outside. When the men had filed out, Anthony said, "We're interested in exactly what you did as executioners of Jesus. Either one of you may begin."

"I'll start," said Latinius. "Nemonius and I were on standby at Golgotha awaiting the arrival of the third prisoner. We had already completed the first part of our assignment. We had just finished placing our earlier arrivals on their crosses. Two dangerous and treasonous thieves they were. All three prisoners were supposed to arrive at the same time, but apparently there was some type of hold up. You know how things go." The gregarious Latinius shrugged and laughed then continued, "There were several soldiers assigned to duty that night. And there were others just hanging out. There were many civilian spectators. We usually get a good crowd, but that day was larger than normal. As always we were on high alert. We have to be on alert and prepared to act because these types of situations are highly volatile. At any moment the crowd could become violent."

Latinius frowned as he struggled to recall the sequence of events.

"Around nine in the morning, the third and final prisoner arrived. This Jesus looked a mess. He was carrying his wooden patibulum with the superscription hanging about his neck. When we got hold of him we laid him down and stretched out his arms across the patibulum. Using sharp spikes we fixed his right hand and then his left. After we accomplished that we affixed ropes to the upright that was already in its place. We attached the wooden patibulum to the ropes and hoisted him right up and into place. This may sound simple, but it is not. The prisoner might be ripped off the wood as you're hoisting him up."

Latinius laughed again, and Marcus and Anthony found themselves wondering how often that occurred.

"Once he is up and in place, we grab his feet, placing them one on top of the other and secure them by driving a spike through the feet and into the upright. There is a pegma attached to the upright, which allows a criminal to support his body weight. The criminal is able to rest his buttocks on it. We allow them this comfort to prevent them from tearing their hands free from the cross and making a mess. We always double check our work to make sure there are no mistakes and the body is secured."

Anthony and Marcus privately doubted Latinius's assurance of always double checking, but they allowed the man to continue without interruption.

"While he was hanging there," Latinius said, "one of the guards gave me the superscription, the one that earlier was around his neck. It read, 'This is Jesus the King of the Jews.' I nailed the sign above his head on the upright. And that's about it. We stood guard. We had a little fun. It didn't take long, maybe six hours, and he died. End of story."

Anthony nodded and asked, "How do you confirm whether the prisoner is dead as opposed to being unconscious?"

Smiling confidently Latinius replied, "Oh, you know he's dead. The body slumps down, and you can hear the prisoner's last gasp of air, then he stops breathing. From the moment he arrived I knew he wasn't going to last long. In fact we had bets among ourselves on how long he would last. Actually, we couldn't believe he was able to make it as far as he did. When I tell you that he was beat up, that's an understatement. He didn't look human. In any event, one of our procedures is breaking the legs of the prisoners to expedite death. If we want to prolong death we leave them as they are. At this scene we were ordered to break the legs of all the prisoners."

Smiling, Anthony asked, "So, did your men break the prisoner's legs?"

"Yes."

Looking intently at Latinius, Anthony asked, "Are you sure? Did you witness their legs being broken?"

Shooting a nervous look at Nemonius, Latinius asked, "Didn't you break their legs?"

Nemonius responded defensively, "What do you mean, did I break their legs? You did not specifically order me to that task. I was not responsible for breaking their legs. What are you insinuating?"

Raising his voice Anthony forcefully interrupted, "Calm down, both of you. No one is accusing or insinuating anything. I'm sure one of the guards in your squad actually broke his legs."

Looking at Latinius Anthony asked, "Was this a direct order to a specific guard or just a general order for anyone to complete?"

Disgusted, Latinius responded, "It doesn't work that way. I looked toward the group of soldiers, some were standing around, others were casting lots for the prisoners' clothes, and I gave the order. When I gave the order several of them stood up and went to the prisoners. I assumed they followed their orders. Why would I think otherwise? I did not watch every move they made. After I gave the order I attended to other responsibilities. There were loud and boisterous people in the crowd that I had to concern myself with. Look, I didn't do anything wrong."

Anthony nodded. "We are merely attempting to ascertain all the facts concerning the execution of these prisoners, specifically this Jesus of Nazareth. If there's nothing more that either of you can add, you are free to go. When you leave, tell the other four soldiers to proceed in. I'm sure that one of the four followed the order. Once we determine who did what, we will be finished here."

As the soldiers exited, Anthony turned to Marcus. "They're a nervous wreck. They seem to think they are in trouble."

"What do you expect?" Marcus asked. "Put yourself in their boots. They've been executing prisoners for years with no questions asked. Now out of nowhere we show up and tell them that we have been ordered by the governor to investigate the death of one of the prisoners they executed. I might be suspicious if I were in their place. In any event I'm willing to bet that the next group will be able to answer our questions."

The four soldiers entered the room. Marcus and Anthony looked at them pleasantly, to set them at ease, and requested that they relax.

"Brothers," Marcus began, "we are attempting to determine a very simple fact. Did this Jesus die on the cross? I know that this must sound foolish to you; however, we have been ordered to determine this fact. You are not in any trouble at this point. The sooner we determine what occurred the sooner we will be gone. Now then, who would like to explain his participation in this event? Anyone can begin."

Petilluis reported that he was ordered to Golgotha for security reasons.

"I was ordered to be on alert for any troublemakers," he said.

Petilluis related the nailing of Jesus to the cross just as Latinuis had stated.

"After he was hanging for about three hours, the weather suddenly changed. It was noon, and the sun was directly overhead. But suddenly the sky became dark as if night had fallen. It stayed that way until he died, about three hours." Petilluis paused, and then continued, "This Jesus was most uncommon. I mean, all the criminals I've ever dealt with become loud and belligerent when they're on that cross. They curse us with every curse imaginable. Or they cry from being consumed with fear. In fact the other two prisoners were cursing and accusing. But in the middle of all that abuse not an angry word came out of this Jesus' mouth. Then, something amusing happened." Petilluis glanced around the room.

"All right," Marcus said, "tell us what happened."

"One of the prisoners was heaping insults at Jesus, telling him to save himself and them, as he had supposedly saved others. Then the prisoner on the other side suddenly tells the first man to shut up. Then he says to Jesus, 'We deserve this death, but you don't. Would you remember me when you come into your kingdom?'"

Petilluis laughed hysterically, and the others joined in, except for one soldier who remained quiet and sober. "But that's not all!" Petilluis's voice was hoarse with laughter. "This Jesus, all bloody and beaten, in the worst shape I've ever seen anybody; he says with all confidence and calmness, 'Truly I say to you, today you shall be with me in paradise.'"

The men rocked with laughter.

"Were those his last words?" asked Marcus.

"No," Petilluis replied. "He said something like, 'Father, into your hands I commit my spirit.' Then he breathed his last breath."

"So which one of you broke his legs?" Anthony demanded.

Quickly Petilluis responded, "It sure wasn't Felix." With that outburst all the soldiers began laughing loudly, smacking one another on the back, and smirking at Felix. Felix sprang out of his chair and attacked Petilluis. The two men grabbed and punched at each other until Felix drew back and brought his sword to Petilluis's chest.

Marcus sprang between them. "Stand down, soldier. What's going on? Are you out of your minds? Stand at attention. If you make one move toward each other, I'll have you arrested and charged with insubordination. Got that? Do you understand me?"

Before he had even finished, the soldiers responded in the affirmative, and all four stood at attention.

Shouting, Anthony asked, "What was that about? Why did you attack your brother, soldier? I want an answer."

"He's not my brother," Felix responded angrily. "None of them are my brothers!"

"You got that right," Petilluis interjected. "His brothers are Jews now. Aren't they?"

With that comment it appeared that the four soldiers were all going to go at it again. Seeing what was about to occur, Marcus grabbed Petilluis and ordered him out of the room.

"I've had enough of your arrogance. You stand by outside, and when we're finished in here we will deal with you."

As he was leaving Petilluis blurted out, "He is the arrogant one. He attacked me. He's the little Jew convert."

When he finally exited the room, Marcus calmly turned to the others and said, "Take a seat."

Reluctantly the soldiers sat down. They stared at the ground, and the tension was almost palpable. Marcus waited, and Felix finally muttered, "I witnessed every event that took place that night."

Marcus drew in his breath and hoped that Felix's account would be brief and to the point. "Go on," he said. "Let's get all the facts out so that we can all get out of here."

"I arrived at the detail at Golgotha, and I was awaiting the arrival of three prisoners who were sentenced to death by crucifixion. The first two arrived. The guards assigned to them turned them over to my squad. Within ten minutes the prisoners were hanging on their crosses. We are very efficient. Then the other prisoner arrived."

While watching the crowd for signs of trouble, Felix had also kept an eye on Jesus. He had observed one of the mob take a dripping rag to Jesus, squeezing the rag's moisture into the mouth of the prisoner.

"I called out to him," Felix said, "and the civilian scurried back to his group. It was evident that this group was very antagonistic toward Jesus. I was able to identify some of them by their dress. They were the elders and priests from the Jewish Temple. They were yelling all sorts of accusations at him. This went on for hours."

Felix related the strangeness of the darkening sky as Latinius had done. "It was evident that something out of the ordinary was happening. The crowd appeared to be frightened and confused. They began looking up in anticipation of something occurring. I felt my senses go on high alert.

"Then I became aware of another group of civilians. They appeared to be his followers. They spoke and dressed as Galileans. They were mostly women and were weeping and waling. They made their way up to his cross, and they stood by watching him suffer. Further away in the darkness I perceived that there were others. I believe that they too were his followers, but they were frightened and hid themselves in the darkness. When I gazed back toward Jesus I overheard him tell one of the men standing with the women to take care of his mother."

With a barely concealed look of disgust, Felix told about the soldiers casting lots for the prisoners' clothes, as Petilluis had stated. He told about Jesus' vesture, which was seamless and therefore worth a little money, so the soldiers did not want to tear it to pieces.

When Felix told of the conversation between Jesus and the other prisoner, he said, "You had to be there to understand the strength of his words. He spoke with such conviction that my heart stirred within me. Then his eyes gazed upward, and I heard him say, 'Father, forgive them because they don't know what they are doing.'" Felix paused. "I heard him say he was thirsty. Some bystanders mimicked his request. Then some of them proceeded over to a jar of sour wine, soaked a sponge in it, put it on a hyssop branch, and pressed it to his mouth while they laughed."

Again, Felix paused and collected himself before going on.

"I must tell you, Marcus, Anthony, I am a veteran soldier. I have fought many battles for Rome. I have witnessed death and destruction throughout my life. And nothing has affected me as much as my witnessing this man's execution."

Clearing his throat, Felix returned to the account of events. "Then he cried out, 'Father, why have you forsaken me?' The earth began to shake. He cried out with the last of his strength; 'It is finished.' And he breathed his last. When the crowds witnessed this last event, the shaking of the earth and his crying out, you could see that they were gripped with fear.

"Finally, I heard the order given to break the prisoners' legs. I observed Varius and Victor approach the criminals. Varius had a heavy hammer in his hand. It's a standard issue used for such purposes. He violently swung it at the hip of the criminal on the left of Jesus. I heard the bones shatter. The prisoner slumped forward and died shortly thereafter. At the same time I observed Victor approach Jesus. He yelled over that he was already dead. Then I witnessed him take his spear and plunge it into Jesus' side. The body hung motionless. Blood and clear fluid dripped down his side and onto his leg. Then Varius approached the criminal to Jesus' right and smashed his hip socket. Within a few minutes he died. And that's everything that I witnessed."

Felix looked steadily at the two interrogators. "I can assure you this Jesus was dead. And he was dead before the other two. His legs were not broken because there was no need."

Anthony turned to Victor and Varius and asked, "Is what Felix said accurate?"

With a smirk on his face and staring directly at Felix, Varius responded, "Yes! He was as dead as the beheaded baptizer." The other soldiers chuckled. "Felix here now worships the fraud!" Varius added, mockingly.

Felix stood up. His eyes blazed, ready for battle, and he said, "I've been with this army longer than any of you. I have been awarded the highest medals that one can receive. I fear no man. But I do fear the consequences of what I participated in. And I am not afraid or ashamed to say that this Jesus was innocent. I don't know much about the gods—his god or ours. But I do know this.. .If there are gods, he was one of them. And I take no pleasure in what I have done."

Marcus spoke. "Our mission was to confirm that Jesus was in fact dead when he was removed from the cross. Our report will indicate that fact and that you performed your assignments with the utmost professionalism." Looking at Anthony Marcus said, "Let us take our leave."

• • •

As Marcus and Anthony exited the garrison, Anthony asked, "What do you think?"

Shrugging his shoulders, Marcus responded, "About what?" He smiled. "I think that they handled their assignment properly. We wanted to establish Jesus' death, and we did."

Nodding, Anthony responded, "I don't mean that. Of course he's dead. I'm talking about the investigation in general. Where do we go from here? There are still many unanswered questions. I'm just wondering what our next move is."

"We have eliminated the theory that he was alive. Therefore, if there was a conspiracy to steal the body, Jesus did not assist. I would prefer to speak with the guards that were assigned to the tomb, but that's going to have to wait. We will round up his disciples and squeeze the truth out of them."

"Yes!" Anthony concurred excitedly. "I think we should start with Joseph of Arimathea. Since it is his tomb, he is a prime suspect. It shouldn't be hard to locate him. He is a temple elder, so he's probably there. If not, I'm sure they can direct us to his residence."

Marcus marched quickly to the horses with Anthony a step behind. When they approached their horses, Marcus mounted and responded to the question Anthony asked moments earlier.

"That's a good starting point. He is the one who assisted in removing the body from the cross. We must include the mother of Jesus. Felix said she was there with other women. We will probably recover the body as soon as we get them in custody and put some pressure on them. I would like to get to the bottom of this today."

Marcus ordered Anthony to get an estimated time of arrival for the soldiers that were dispatched to Joppa.

Anthony confirmed that they should be back within days, and Felix would let them know of their return.

With that information they proceeded in the direction of Arimathea.

Interrogation of Joseph

Marcus was irritated. He was hoping to clear this case within a few days. Now this day had started late, and the interviews at the garrison had not been as simple as he had anticipated. Just before the midnight hour, he and Anthony were approaching Jerusalem—what the Jews called the old City of David.

They entered the city by passing through the high, thick, gray stone wall that encircled Jerusalem. The city itself had been transformed by Herod the Great, and there were many palaces, citadels, and public monuments. Atop an enormous white stone platform stood the temple in its entire, glorious splendor. Because it was nighttime the temple's glitter was hidden.

They arrived at the front gate of the temple and secured their horses. As they walked up the many steps, Anthony wondered if they would find anyone awake and about at this hour. No sooner had the thought taken shape in his mind than the men were greeted by a Jewish priest rushing past.

The priest, in spite of his haste, slowed his steps and asked with curiosity, "May I assist you soldiers? Is there something I can do for you?"

Anthony responded, "Yes, you can. We are attempting to locate Joseph of Arimathea. We were informed that we might find him at the temple."

The priest looked thoughtful for a moment, and then he responded quietly, "Yes, usually he's here but not this late at night. May I inquire as to why you wish to speak to him? Is there something I can help you with?"

Abruptly Anthony answered, "No. We need to speak with him. If he's not here, where can we locate him?"

The priest pointed toward Arimathea, a city in the Judean hills northwest of Jerusalem. That part of the country was home to the rich and powerful Jewish families and high-ranking Roman officials.

"He lives straight up that road. If you follow this road you will come to white marble mansions and palaces built around courtyards with elaborate gardens and pools. You will come to a grape orchard on the north side of the road. His home will be located on the south side of the road right before the orchard ends. It will be the first house you come to."

"Are you a personal friend of Joseph?" Marcus asked.

"Yes," replied the priest, "I know him well. He is an honorable counselor, a devout man who serves in the temple. He is a member of the Sanhedrin. He is one of our most respected leaders."

"Yes, yes, yes! All you Jews are honorable. We want to question him and anyone else who was a follower of Jesus. The governor has given us the power to arrest anyone we deem involved or withholding knowledge pertinent to our investigation. Are you a follower of Jesus, the one who was crucified last Friday?"

Startled by the question, the priest said, "No, no, never. He was just another false prophet."

Firing out another question, Marcus asked, "Is Joseph a follower of Jesus?"

Shaking his head, the priest answered, "I'm not sure what you mean. I know he was aware of Jesus. As we all were. But whether he was a follower I can't answer that with certainty."

Bending toward the priest, Marcus continued his aggressive questioning. "Are there any other priests, elders, sympathetic to this Jesus?"

Visibly trembling, the priest said, "One of his best friends was Nicodemus. He also is a member of the counsel. I don't know if Nicodemus was a follower. These men are very busy men. They are in and out of the temple and are always assisting our people in the community. I believe they were sympathetic toward him. But I cannot speak for them."

Glaring directly into the priest's eyes, Marcus growled, "Do you have any direct knowledge of this Jesus or his followers?"

"Not direct knowledge, only hearsay. And I know the hearsay is false. For example, this Jesus claimed to be the Messiah. The Son of God. The anointed one. Our Scriptures teach that the Messiah will come and restore his people and establish his kingdom. He neither established God's kingdom nor restored his people." The priest looked resignedly at the two soldiers. "As you know, he was crucified. Regarding his followers, I've heard they are uneducated fishermen. That's all I know concerning them."

The priest took a few steps and then turned to add, "Except that they all ran when Jesus was arrested."

Acknowledging the information with a curt nod, Marcus said, "We will be back. If we determine that you have withheld information we will cut your tongue out."

• • •

The sun had not yet risen when the two men found themselves standing at the door of the house of Joseph. In answer to their knocking, the door swung open to reveal an elderly couple, a man and his wife. They were dressed in their nightclothes, white tunics made of fine linen. Marcus and Anthony could see the fear on their faces at being disturbed before dawn.

"Who goes there?" queried the elderly gentleman. "What is it that you want? Please do not cause us harm."

"We are not here to inflict harm. We are here to speak with the one known as Joseph of Arimathea. Bring him here directly," ordered Marcus.

"I am Joseph," he said, and he stroked his long white beard.

The men followed the couple into the house. The woman left the men to return to the bedchamber, but Joseph walked down the long, tiled corridor and entered a room. The walls of the room were lined with cabinets, behind which were scrolls. Joseph motioned the soldiers to sit at a nearby table.

"Here. Sit. May I offer you a glass of wine?"

Marcus and Anthony smiled gratefully. "Yes," said Marcus. "We would appreciate that. I am Marcus, and this is Anthony. We have been ordered to investigate the disappearance of the body of Jesus of Nazareth from your tomb. We have questions concerning your relationship with Jesus. We have information that you were there at his crucifixion."

After the wine was poured and the three men had tossed back the first deep swallow, Marcus resumed speaking.

"Joseph, are you aware that his body is missing?" "Yes, I heard a rumor, but I don't know anything about it."

"What was your relationship to Jesus, and when did it begin?"

Sitting back in his chair, Joseph thought for a moment before responding. He stroked his beard absently, and Marcus recognized an unconscious habit in the old man. Marcus had been skillful at recognizing deception through body language. He was taught that although a suspect may sound truthful his body will always give him away. The fact that Joseph stroked his beard and gazed up, looking toward his right led Marcus to believe that he was about to hear the truth.

After a few minutes, Joseph said, "I was first introduced to Jesus by my friend Nicodemus. Nicodemus and I both serve on the counsel—the Jewish counsel, at the Temple in Jerusalem." Lowering his voice, Joseph asked, "Are you familiar with the Jewish faith?"

"We're not interested in your faith," said Anthony. "We are interested in your relationship to Jesus."

Lifting his hands as if in prayer, Joseph spoke softly, "Yes, I understand. But I must speak of our faith in order to answer your question. That is the only way I can explain my relationship with Jesus." Joseph paused, awaiting a comment, but when none was forthcoming, he asked, "May I continue?"

"Continue."

"In our sacred text, God promised us a Messiah. One who would come and establish his kingdom on earth. For hundreds of years the Jewish people have been waiting with anticipation for his arrival. Over the years there have been many who have claimed to be this Messiah. It has always turned out to be a false claim. Approximately three years ago Jesus began his ministry. It was reported to us, the Sanhedrin, that Jesus was performing signs and wonders that no man could do without God's power. It was reported that he was healing the sick and feeding the poor and hungry. When we heard of such wonders we questioned the people who were reporting them. In all the cases it appeared that they were without exaggeration. As leaders in the Hebrew community, the Sanhedrin had the duty and the responsibility to examine such claims."

Marcus knew that, among the Jewish people, the Sanhedrin was the highest ruling body and court of justice. The members had the authority to make judgments regarding conflicts within the Jewish community. This ruling counsel had its own law enforcement, the temple guards. The Sanhedrin exercised authority over religious, civil, and criminal matters unhindered by Rome, to a certain extent.

"With all due respect," Joseph said, inclining his head at the men, "we have been in bondage to Rome for many years, and before that there were other empires. We have prayed for the day that God's promise of redemption would be revealed. I was introduced to Jesus by my friend, who seemed to be impressed with his message. After meeting him myself, I, too, was intrigued by him. Nicodemus and I often sided against the other priests and elders, who envied the recognition and power that the people were bestowing upon him."

Joseph frowned and shook his head. Pulling at his beard, he continued, "The things that Jesus said concerning who he was and where he came from disturbed many of the leaders, including me. My brothers closed their minds to his messages and lectures. There were many arguments among us. I must admit I was a coward and did not speak up when I should have." Joseph shifted in his seat. "In the last week, before his crucifixion, there was heated discussion. Many were wondering what to do about Jesus. Neither I nor Nicodemus realized until it was too late that the Sanhedrin, led by Caiaphas and his advisors, had plotted to eliminate Jesus once and for all."

Joseph turned in his seat to face the men.

"Well, you know the rest. After he was condemned to death and crucified on the cross, Nicodemus and I requested his body. Before we were permitted to remove him, Pilate wanted confirmation from his soldiers that he was dead. After he received that information he allowed us to take Jesus. Because the preparation for our Sabbath was at hand and my tomb was close by, I offered it for the burial of Jesus."

Joseph then elaborated on the exact procedures of the Jews in their burial customs.

"It is imperative that the body is unstained. After we wash the body and it is clean of all stain, we use myrrh and aloes. The aloes help in cleaning and restoring the body. The myrrh has a pungent nature and overpowers any other odors. Then we wrap the body in linens. We use a roller in order to keep the wrapping as tight as skin on the body. Lastly, we place a napkin over the deceased's head and face."

Marcus asked, "Who assisted you and Nicodemus?"

"His mother, his cousin John, a follower named Mary Magdalene. There were others; I'm not sure who they were. We hurried to finish before sunset—before our Sabbath. We completed as best we could, and the Roman guards and temple guards rolled the stone against the entrance of the tomb and sealed it with the Roman seal."

"When did you become aware of the body being missing?" asked Anthony.

Joseph responded nervously, "I heard. I believe it was late Sunday afternoon, the day after the Sabbath. Some of the chief priests returned to the temple and stated that the body was missing. They were quite concerned. Caiaphas met with them privately. He would not allow me to attend this meeting. When they left his chambers, they all in one accord stated that the disciples stole the body while the temple guards and the Roman guards were asleep."

"What did you do when you were informed that the body was missing? Did you do anything?" Marcus could not keep the heat out of his voice.

The elderly man looked frightened. "I wasn't sure what to do. At first I did not believe the report. As far as I was concerned, it was simply out of the question that someone could have stolen the body. I knew guards were assigned. There was no possible way, even if the guards were asleep, that anyone would have been able to reopen the tomb without alerting the guards." Looking meaningfully at the men, Joseph said, "I know for a fact the temple guards were specifically assigned to keep watch. There is no way that they would have not carried out their assignment, especially in this circumstance."

Ruefully, the old man added, "Even the idea of his disciples attempting to remove the body is preposterous. All of them were scared for their lives. One of their strongest leaders, called Peter, ran away in tears just prior to Jesus' crucifixion."

"Where were you Saturday night and Sunday morning?" asked Marcus.

"After we prepared the body I went home for the Sabbath. Sunday afternoon I returned to the temple where, as I said earlier, I was informed the body had been stolen."

Anthony asked, "Can anyone corroborate your testimony regarding your whereabouts?"

Thinking of his wife, who would be making bread by now, he nodded. "Of course. My wife was here with me. And there were other priests at the temple."

"Joseph, what have you heard since then?" asked Marcus.

"I have heard wonderful things." Joseph looked anxiously at the men. "I have heard that he has risen. I have heard that he has appeared to many of his disciples. It wasn't until I heard these reports that I recalled his words. He promised he would rise on the third day. I did not realize then because he spoke in parables, but I understand now. He said that if this temple were destroyed he would raise it up in three days. When he said this we thought that he meant the great Temple in Jerusalem, which was mad. But he meant his body." There was an unnatural light in the old man's eyes as he said, "The Messiah is alive."

Marcus angrily rebuked the man. "*Silence!* I'm not interested in your Jewish nonsense. Where can we find Nicodemus, Peter, and John?"

Joseph directed the men to the temple for Nicodemus and to the home of John's mother in the lower part of the Old City.

As the soldiers took their leave from the house, Joseph put his arm around his wife and together they watched the horses galloping back toward Jerusalem.

"My dear," said Joseph, "whoever is going to believe the truth?"

John and the Followers

Famished and exhausted, Marcus and Anthony proceeded to Anthony's home. They discussed the testimony that Joseph had provided. They both concluded that he seemed to be a reliable witness. They were sure that he would neither have the strength or the courage to be involved in this theft.

When they arrived they stumbled into the warmth of the little house once again and collapsed at the low table. Like starving wolves, they attacked and devoured all the food that Madelyn placed before them. When every morsel had disappeared and they were struggling to hold their heads upright, they made their way to their beds and were sound asleep before they could remove their belts.

Madelyn called for Ruth's assistance. While she tended to her husband and made him comfortable for the night, she sent Ruth to Marcus.

The Jewish girl stood in the doorway of the guest bedroom and found herself blushing furiously. Removing Marcus's outer accouterments and boots should not have this effect on her. As a servant she often was called upon to remove the shoes and boots of the men who visited the home and to wash their filthy feet. Sometimes she would wash their hair as well. But with this man, Ruth was suddenly aware of the intimacy of her actions, and she was overwhelmed by her feelings.

"Is there a problem?"

Startled, Ruth turned to find Madelyn standing behind her.

"I am fine. I am just about finished preparing his room."

Madelyn watched for a few moments and knew she had never seen Ruth perform these ministrations in quite this way before. She wondered if Marcus were at all aware.

When Ruth had finished, she bowed toward Marcus and began to exit the room.

Marcus, not wanting to miss the opportunity to talk with Ruth, shouted, "Ruth! It is a beautiful night. The stars seem brighter." Embarrassed by his stumbling over the words he smiled and said, "Ruth, would you like to take a walk tonight?"

"I was hoping…Yes," Ruth said and smiled.

Marcus and Ruth walked and talked most of the moonlit night. Marcus shared memories of his life, and Ruth was in awe of everything she heard. Joy had filled Marcus's heart as they laughed and conversed. Ruth imagined the possibilities.

Holding Marcus by the arm, Ruth whispered, "You have a long day ahead of you. Go, rest, I will see you in the morning."

Marcus and Ruth stopped at his room, stared at each other, and passionately kissed. Marcus took a deep breath as he entered his room. As he lay on his bed, a sweet peace fell over him.

• • •

Shivering in the predawn hour and stamping his feet to restore circulation to his sluggish muscles, Marcus felt satisfied, along with something else he couldn't quite identify. The investigation was proceeding with some unexpected surprises, but he felt they were making progress nonetheless. His stomach was full, and his body had again experienced the deep and peaceful slumber that had been eluding him for a long time now. And he was especially pleased to be starting the day at a more appropriate time. They should get much accomplished today.

As Marcus saddled his horse, he looked up and caught a glimpse of the young servant girl, Ruth, as she was ducking into the house with a jug of water. In the starlight, she had only been a wisp of a shadow, but he knew it was her. He recognized the graceful movement of her slim hips and the whiteness of her long, tapering fingers as they held the ears of the clay jug. The skin on his arms burned, and he rubbed it vigorously. He looked forward to his return.

Arriving back in the Old City, Marcus and Anthony pushed their horses through the crowded streets. According to Joseph, they would find the cousin of Jesus at a house beyond the temple, so they made their way toward the magnificent edifice. Even soldiers of pagan Rome, which was steeped in majestic grandeur and ostentatious luxury, were awed by the splendor of the Jewish Temple.

In daylight, reflecting the rays of the sun, the enormous walls glittered and glowed with the colors of the rainbow—appearing white or blue or pink or yellow.

The size alone of the many-dimensional building was breathtaking.

Marcus knew that as an Edomite (a descendant of Jacob's twin brother, Esau), Herod was not considered a Jew by the descendants of the twelve tribes of Israel. Herod had rebuilt the second Temple in Jerusalem in an attempt to gain greater acceptance. Marcus didn't think his effort had increased the king's popularity, although it had certainly resulted in a house for their God that inspired wonder, reverence, and admiration.

"It is a worthy temple for a god," Marcus commented, grudgingly. He harbored ill feelings toward the Jewish God, and this investigation into his supposed messiah was adding to Marcus's frustration with the mystical religion. But he was astonished to feel a softening in his chest, and he saw the image of Ruth pass quickly across his vision.

Anthony only nodded in response, and soon the two men found themselves winding through the dusty maze of the Jerusalem streets and alleys. Snaking uphill and down, the roadways caused the multitude to walk at a tilt and hunch their bodies in order to keep from falling over. Gradually, they located the small market Joseph had described. Open-air shops that housed craftsmen, potters, and bakers lined the road. In the center was a colorful bazaar featuring fruits and vegetables, dried fish, perfumes, and jewelry. The smell of fresh-cooked food was inviting, and the men decided to eat. They were not far from the house now.

After a quick meal of barley, bread, and fish, Anthony flipped a coin to the perfume merchant and slipped a tiny glass flask into his shirt. The perfume would make a nice gift for Madelyn. Marcus pretended not to notice.

Continuing north on the road, the house situated on a knoll came into view. At the door they were met by a handsome young man in a fine tunic.

"Greetings. My name is John, a follower of Jesus the Master," he said. "I have already been informed that you are inquiring about my master and his followers. How may I assist?"

In a condescending tone Anthony responded, "Rumors travel fast. Let me get right to the point. We are in fact attempting to recover the stolen body of Jesus. And we expect you to lead us to him. We can assure you that if you cooperate your life will not be put in jeopardy. However, if we find out that you have lied or have not been completely truthful, the power and authority of Rome will be used in all its strength against you and the rest of the followers. We will crush you. Destroy your homes and make slaves of your families. I'm sure you understand the ramifications?"

John smiled. "Yes, I do understand. I can lead you to him if you're willing."

Adrenaline raced through the veins of Marcus and Anthony. Finally they would be able to recover the body and complete the investigation. They did not realize that John meant something very different.

John spoke again. "May I ask you a question? Did you interview your guards that were assigned to watch the tomb?"

Sparked by anger, Marcus responded, "No, you may not ask. We ask the questions, and you answer. This is not a game. We don't have time for this. We have determined that you are one of the followers of Jesus and a leader within your group. We are convinced that you have answers. We will not go back and forth regarding this matter. You will tell the truth or you will accompany us back to the garrison where we will extract the information from you."

The Master Jesus had nicknamed John and his brother, James, "Sons of Thunder," and the nickname had been apt. With his customary boldness and brusque bluntness, John said, "Are you interested in the truth? The truth may not be what you want to hear."

Anthony turned to Marcus and said aggressively, "He has admitted to knowing where the body is. Let's arrest him and bring him back with us. I'm sick and tired of this charade. Just give me a few minutes with him, and he'll be squealing like a pig."

Marcus had not taken his eyes from John. He asked him, "What exactly do you mean, are we interested in the truth? What is it that you want to say?"

Displaying a confident manner, John answered, "We all have our perspective regarding what is true and real. Because someone believes something does not necessarily make it true. I spent the last three years as a follower of Jesus. I have seen things that most men will never see this side of heaven. I was at the crucifixion from beginning to end. And what I witnessed confirmed what I already knew to be true. Jesus was much more than a man. He was in fact the Son of God."

John continued to speak without pause while he walked outside to a nearby garden. The soldiers were compelled to follow.

"Before the foundation of the world, God planned all that has occurred. I do not wish to anger you, and I am not making little of your investigation. I realize from all outward appearances it seems that the body of Jesus was removed by human hands. I am simply asking whether you are open to another possibility. Are you really interested in the truth, or do you just want to prove your theory?"

John seated himself on a bench and motioned for the soldiers to do likewise.

"I asked about the guards because they are witnesses to what occurred at the tomb. In fact your guards are witnesses to everything that occurred from the day of His crucifixion until the morning of his resurrection."

"Resurrection? Marcus and Anthony uttered the word simultaneously.

John went on as though they had not spoken.

"They may find it hard to explain or understand, nevertheless they witnessed something miraculous. If they are truthful they will testify that something happened beyond their human understanding. Have you questioned them?"

Anthony said, "They have been temporarily assigned to another province. They will be questioned very soon. Look, we will not debate—"

"If you started your investigation at the tomb I'm sure you noticed a troubling scene, a scene most difficult to explain," John said. "I know the Pharisees have devised a scheme to explain away the missing body. They allege that the guards fell asleep, and we, his followers, stole the body."

With wry sarcasm, Marcus said, "Yes, so we've heard."

Raising his palms, John said, "Please, I am not attempting to provoke you to anger. What took place at Joseph's tomb is the most important event in the history of man. Your investigation will not prove otherwise."

"Stop right there," said Marcus. "The one who you say was sent by God was turned over to Roman authority, and we determined his fate. That's a fact that cannot be disputed. If he was not of this world and sent by God as you claim, where was this God when he was scourged and crucified? I understand from testimony of those that witnessed the event that he called on his God from the cross and was not answered. Some have suggested that he was an innocent man, even a good man; however, neither he nor his God could stop the execution." Marcus stood up, staring arrogantly into John's eyes. Punching his fist into his hand, Marcus roared, "Roman authority sentenced him to death and determined his fate!"

John gently rose out of his chair and whispered, "What would it take for you to consider that my master was not of this world—that he himself directed these events? What if I could prove that all that occurred was predetermined by God and revealed to his people through our Scriptures?"

Marcus settled himself and sat back down, and John followed.

"I do not wish to discuss religion. My goal is to retrieve his body and determine who's involved in its theft," said Marcus.

John pleaded, "Marcus, you will never be able to retrieve his body. He has risen, and I bear witness of this fact. And I am not alone. He has appeared several times to his followers. Let me prove to you from our sacred writings that his birth, death, and resurrection were prophesied. You are a reasonable person; if after you hear my argument you find contradiction, you can do what you please to me."

"I will do what I please with you in any case." Marcus thought, *If I show some interest maybe he will be more inclined to reveal the truth.* "I am in a merciful mood, so you may continue."

"You will not be disappointed. Our ancient texts contain prophecies that were forecasted hundreds, even thousands, of years before Jesus was born, but they tell the details of his life. These intricate aspects cannot be disputed. It appears to you that events were dictated by the power of Rome, but I will prove to you that the events and power were in the hands of God." John spread his hands wide, then brought them back and clasped them, interlacing his fingers. "Yes, there was evil intent by both the Romans and the Jewish leaders. Certainly they are responsible for their actions." John eyed Marcus and Anthony. "Your own people found no fault in him."

Anthony and Marcus looked at each other. They were astonished and impressed by John's boldness. He spoke as one sure of his message.

When John stood and returned to the house, the soldiers trailed behind him. Inside, John led them to a room with a low table at the center. On the table were several scrolls.

With a wave of his hands, John indicated that the men should seat themselves around the table.

"I gained permission to borrow these sacred scrolls because Annas is a distant relative of my mother. I have been reviewing the prophecies for myself, and that is why

I am so eager to share this news with you. Though you may not think so, it is necessary for your investigation."

Marcus nodded his head. As part of his network within the Jewish community, he had heard that John and his brother, the sons of Zebedee and Salome, had high connections within the Sanhedrin, and it could go no higher than with the high priests, Annas, and his son-in-law, Caiaphas.

"We will look at just the prophecies that were fulfilled in one day, the day of his crucifixion. That day was predicted more than five centuries ago.

"On the night of Passover, I and the others sat down with Jesus to share our customary meal. The meal itself is significant. We celebrate it to remember the great Exodus of our people out of Egyptian bondage. Before Pharaoh let our people go, God had to send plagues to convince him. A lamb was sacrificed, and its blood was painted on homes of the Hebrew slaves in order to protect them from the tenth plague, which was the death of the firstborn child."

"These events mean nothing to my investigation," said Marcus irritably.

"They mean everything," John argued. "Our Scripture is filled with examples of what would culminate in the sacrifice of our Messiah for the forgiveness of sins. But I see that I must stick directly to the predictions."

John lovingly lifted one of the scrolls and carefully rolled it open upon the table. Although neither Marcus nor Anthony could read the Hebrew text, they leaned in to look at the writing. Against their will, the supernatural element of the story of Jesus was gaining their interest and attention.

"It was at our Passover meal that Jesus stated he was going to be betrayed by one of us. And he was—Judas Iscariot. This prediction was written hundreds of years ago." John read from the text, "'Even my familiar friend in whom I trusted, who ate my bread, has lifted up his heel against me' (Psalm 41:9, NKJV). Judas, who ate with us and shared literally Jesus' bread, betrayed him for thirty pieces of silver. You can easily confirm this by interviewing any of the elders."

Turning again to the scroll, John read:

> Then I said to them, 'If it is agreeable to you, give me my wages; and if not refrain.' So they weighed out for my wages thirty pieces of silver. So I took the thirty pieces of silver and threw them into the house of the Lord for the potter.
> Zachariah 11:12, 13 (NKJV)

"Judas took the money and later attempted to return it to the elders. They refused it, rejected it, so he threw it at them. The money could not be returned to the temple treasury because it was blood money, so it was used to buy the potter's field where Judas hung himself, and where he is now buried."

Lifting his eyes to gaze at the men, John said, "These prophecies are specific." Counting on his fingers, which he held aloft, John went on, "One, betrayed by a friend. Two, for thirty pieces of silver, not gold. Three, the silver was not placed down but thrown down in the house of the Lord. Four, the money was used to buy a potter's field."

The soldiers stared at John in dumbfounded amazement, and the young man continued, "That night, Jesus was forsaken by us, his disciples. I have a problem even thinking about that night, but it cannot be denied. We were afraid, and we ran." John read, "'Strike the Shepherd, and the sheep will be scattered' (Zachariah 13:7, NKJV). That was us. We scattered when they arrested Jesus. We were terrified, and we deserted him. Useless, we were. We left him to suffer alone." John's eyes filled with tears, and he coughed to clear his throat before continuing. "The priests produced false witnesses. Pilate saw through all of that, yet he refused to intervene. This also was predicted." Pointing to a place on the scroll, John read, "'Fierce witnesses rise up; they ask me things I do not know' (Psalm 35:11, NKJV). Jesus was silent before his accusers as it is written here in Isaiah, 'He was oppressed and afflicted, yet he opened not his mouth' (Isaiah 53:7, NKJV). Now the predictions become more compelling. You know what type of suffering a man goes through when being scourged and then crucified. If the temple elders could have sentenced Jesus to death, it would have been by stoning. Stoning is the Jewish mode of execution for crimes worthy of death. But the prophecy foretold that the anointed one would be *crucified*!" John's voice rose in excitement. "How could the prophets know that the anointed one would come when Rome would control the mode of execution?" John read again, "'He was wounded for our transgressions, he was bruised for our iniquities; the chastisement for our peace was upon him, and by his stripes we are healed' (Isaiah 53:5, NKJV). On the day of the crucifixion, at the insistence of the chief priest and elders, Pilate released Barabbas and scourged Jesus, which culminated in his being nailed, pierced, through his hands and feet, onto the cross. Prior to that he was smitten and spit upon."

John turned to the scroll once again.

"'I gave my back to those who struck me, and my cheeks to those who pluck out my beard; I did not hide my face from shame and spitting' (Isaiah 50:7, NKJV). They punched him, and they mocked him, and the Scriptures would be fulfilled:

> All who see me ridicule me; they shoot out the lip, they shake their head, saying, 'He trusted in the Lord; let Him rescue Him; let Him deliver Him, since he delights in Him!
> Psalm 22:7, 8 (NKJV)
> My knees are weak through fasting; and my flesh is feeble from lack of fatness. I also have become a reproach to them; when they look at me they shake their head.
> Psalm 109:24, 25 (NKJV)

"After Pilate had Jesus whipped and forced him to carry the cross, he was so weak that, under the weight of the cross, his knees were giving way, just as predicted. Your soldiers had to order a citizen to assist him in carrying the cross. When he finally reached the Place of the Skull, where he would be crucified, he was forced down on the wood, and his hands and feet pierced with spikes. That is clearly foretold, 'They pierced my hands and my feet'" (Zechariah 12:10, NKJV), he read, still pointing at the Scriptures.

"How could a Jewish prophet from that time be able to predict such a fate to the messiah? It is impossible, my friends. And there's much more. It was predicted he would be crucified among transgressors." John read from the scroll, "'Because he poured out his soul unto death and he was numbered with the transgressors' (Isaiah 53:12, NKJV). Two thieves died next to him. In the midst of all the pain Jesus made intersession for his persecutors. It is written, 'And he bore the sin of many, and made intercession for the transgressors'(Isaiah 53:12, NKJV). He cried out for his persecutors. He was hated, rejected, and yet he prayed for them to be forgiven. It is written, 'He is despised and rejected by men, a man of sorrows and acquainted with grief. And we hid, as it were, our faces from him; He was despised and we did not esteem him' (Psalm 69:8, 118:22, NKJV). Pilate will confirm that they hated him without a cause, and our Scriptures predicted it. Here again," and John pointed to the scroll, "'Those who hate me without a cause are more than the hairs of my head' (Isaiah 49:7, NKJV).

"The most crushing memory of all is the one of us, his disciples, running for cover. Filled with fear and trembling. Forgotten were all the miracles. I witnessed him control the very wind and the seas. I watched him feed thousands and heal lepers. I witnessed all the miracles, even the raising of our friend from the dead, forgotten because of fear. After he was arrested his friends stood afar off." John's eyes were moist as he read the text, "'My loved ones and my friends stand aloof from my plague, and my relatives stand afar off. I also have become a reproach to them; when they look at me, they shake their heads. I can count all my bones. They look and stare at me'" (Psalm 38:11, 109:25, 22:17, NKJV).

Marcus and Anthony were restless. John's enthusiasm was making them both anxious, and they wagged their heads at each other in disbelief as they readjusted their sitting positions, finding it difficult to relax.

Pausing for a moment to collect himself, John inquired, "Did you happen to interview the soldiers assigned to the scene of the crucifixion? The soldiers that sat right under the cross? They were casting lots, gambling."

"Yes," replied Anthony. "They were gambling for his vesture. They had already torn his garments and divided them among themselves. What's your point?"

"You said it correctly, the garments were divided, and they cast lots for his clothing—that valued one-piece vesture that had been wrapped around him. Now consider this writing, 'They divide my garments among them, and for my clothing they cast lots' (Psalm 22:18, NKJV). The garments were parted among the soldiers, but the vesture was awarded to one by the casting of lots.

"And what of this, 'And for my thirst they gave me vinegar to drink' (Psalm 69:21, NKJV). Twice vinegar was offered to him on the cross; first vinegar mixed with gall and myrrh, but when he tasted it he would not drink it for he would not meet his sufferings in a state of stupefaction, which is the effect of myrrh. It's used if the executioners wanted to show mercy. However, when he cried, 'I thirst' (Psalm 69:21, NKJV), vinegar was given him to drink.

"During his suffering Jesus cried out to the Father. To those who witnessed that it may have appeared that Jesus had second thoughts. But those words were the fulfillment of Scripture. You see, at that moment Jesus was being judged for the sins of all mankind. Because of who he is his sacrifice is immeasurable." John read the text, "'My God, My God, why have you forsaken me?'" (Psalm 22:1, NKJV).

Resting his eyes on each man, one at a time, John said, "That is what the Messiah had to feel at that moment, the total separation from fellowship and communion with his Father."

John was no longer reading from the scroll but speaking from memory. "From the cross, Jesus also declared what is written, 'Into your hand I commit my spirit' (Psalm 31:5, NKJV). Jesus said this to demonstrate his control over his own spirit.

"It is also written, 'My heart is like wax; it has melted within me' (Psalm 22:1, NKJV). That may be interpreted in many ways, but when you put all of these prophesies together it is beyond human probability that they could occur within a twenty-four hour period without the power and authority of Almighty God. Our God is sovereign over the events of human history."

Reaching again for the scroll, John said, "Let me mention just four more prophesies that no one can manipulate, and you are witness to some. Isn't it standard procedure to break the legs of the prisoners when they are lingering on the cross? And were not the other prisoners who were next to Jesus dealt with in that way? Not Jesus. I was there and witnessed it. When they came to him he was already dead. To confirm that your soldiers pierced his side. Blood and fluid ran out. Look here in the Scriptures, 'He guards all his bones: not one of them is broken' (Psalm 34:20, NKJV). Who guards his bones?

Almighty God guards his bones. And as it is written by the prophet Zechariah, 'They will look on me whom they pierced'" (Zechariah 12:10, NKJV).

Becoming almost cocky, John asked, "And what about the weather? Our prophet Amos predicted that in that day darkness will fall over the land." John read the text.

"'And it shall come to pass in that day,' says the Lord God, 'that I will make the sun go down at noon, and I will darken the earth in broad daylight'" (Amos 8:9, NKJV).

John peered at the men. "What happened that day? And the tomb? It was foretold the Messiah would be buried in a rich man's tomb. In Isaiah, 'And they made his grave with the wicked and with the rich at his death' (Isaiah 53:9, NKJV).

"How convenient that a rich man at the scene allows his new unused tomb to be used for a prisoner named Jesus. This tomb is conveniently located nearby."

John opened his arms as if to embrace the soldiers and pleaded, "There is so much more that I can testify to. I know how important it is for you to recover the body and so complete your investigation, but it will not end in that manner. There is no body to recover. He has risen, and I believe you must consider my testimony." John's voice grew stronger and more vehement. "If one were inclined they could manipulate some of these prophesies. But clearly most of these events could not be humanly controlled. How he would be betrayed by a friend. How he would suffer and be humiliated. The way he would die. Where he would be buried. How his friends would forsake him. Even the actions of the soldiers assigned to the scene.

"Consider it, my friends. Is it plausible that these events could be controlled by human effort?" Becoming overwhelmed with excitement, John continued, "And who could have planned and manipulated such an elaborate hoax? They would have to control time itself. Even his genealogy is spelled out in the Scriptures. His birth, his life, and death could not have been humanly planned. If you can't see that from what I just testified, then you don't want to see it."

Without warning the men heard a disturbance at the entrance of the house. The soldiers rose and grasped their swords. As they stood prepared to defend themselves, several people rushed into the room. When John realized that the soldiers were about to physically confront the perceived threat, he jumped up and shouted, "No! Stop! They will do you no harm. They are my family and friends."

The group of Jews stared in shock at the soldiers with their drawn swords. John quickly moved between the soldiers and pleaded, "Sit. Everyone, please take a seat." Looking toward Marcus and Anthony, John introduced them as his guests. "Marcus and Anthony, this is James, my brother. This is Andrew and his brother, Simon Peter. This is Mary, the mother of Jesus, and Mary Magdalene, friend and follower of Jesus."

No one made a move, and John continued, "Please let us sit and relax. My friends have just returned from the market. There is plenty of food for all. Stay a while longer and be our dinner guests." John explained to his group the reason for the soldiers' presence.

Marcus was feeling uneasy from the testimony of John, and he did not desire any fruitless conversation with these people. Before he could politely decline, Anthony said, "That sounds good to me."

Marcus glowered at his younger partner, but his efforts were lost on Anthony. John gestured, and the men sat down. Within minutes the women had returned with platters of bread and pots of hot, thick soup.

After the women cleared away the remnants of the meal, they returned with bowls of pickled watermelon rind, green almonds, and walnuts.

Anthony scooped a piece of rind and smacked his lips at the tastiness of the fruit. He licked the juice from his fingers. Marcus scowled and pointed to the water bowls used for cleaning the hands. Anthony smiled and shrugged.

Shifting his attention away from Anthony, Marcus asked, "So, you are Mary, the mother of Jesus, and you are the Peter who is the leader of this group?"

"I am Peter, but I don't know how much of a leader I am," responded the big, burly man. His matted black curls and springy beard were thicker than the wool of a sheep.

"Yes, apparently Jesus' followers aren't much on courage or leadership," Marcus said and smirked.

Peter seemed to fold in on himself, embarrassed by the comment. He felt that his cowardice was known throughout the region. He could not forgive himself for having denied even knowing the Master three times—just as Jesus had predicted he would, no less. Peter wondered if there was still a place for him as a follower of Jesus. Would Jesus still accept him as a disciple? Or was his time as ended as it was for the suicidal Judas?

"Is there something you want to know about, my son?" The question was asked gently but deliberately, and Marcus turned toward the woman. Her dark hair was faded and streaked lightly with gray, but her eyes were piercing; and he felt in them the reprimand for his rudeness toward the hairy giant.

"There is, woman," replied Marcus. "His body is missing, and we have been assigned by the governor of Rome to recover it and arrest the thieves. However, if they are cooperative we may forego the arrest. We have information that you were at the scene on the night in question." Marcus asked these questions as if John's testimony meant nothing.

"Yes," replied Mary. "Where else would I be when my son was crucified?"

Anthony felt an unaccustomed sympathy and said, "We are sorry, but we must ask some difficult questions."

"Where is your son?" Marcus asked abruptly. "If anyone knows, it would be you."

Staring directly into the eyes of Marcus, Mary said, "I understand your impatience with us. You have been assigned an impossible task."

Marcus and Anthony noted how calm and peaceful Mary was in their presence. If she were guilty or had knowledge of the theft, her nervousness would be evident, but she radiated a serene tranquility. The thought occurred to both men that she seemed more like a woman who had seen her son alive, rather than dead. The soldiers exchanged searching looks. Was the incredible testimony of these Jews having a hypnotic effect or could there be more than just a death in this story?

Looking again at Marcus, Mary said, "It is known that deep in your heart you long for the truth. You have acquainted yourself with our religion, our customs, and culture. As surely as the prophecies are true, it was also determined long before we met that you should hear the testimony. Not just the facts concerning your investigation but the answers to the real questions of life. We have those answers, and they are connected to your investigation." Turning to John, Mary said, "Could you please share the Scriptures once more?"

Thinking that the woman intended for John to repeat the information he had earlier shared, Marcus interrupted, "That's not necessary."

"Oh, yes, it is," Mary said. "You have not heard my story."

Marcus looked away and then back at the woman. He nodded, and Mary spoke, "While living in Nazareth a messenger appeared to me. I was very young and engaged to Joseph, a carpenter. This messenger from God explained to me that I had found favor in the sight of God and that I was going to conceive and bear a son. I was to call him Jesus. The messenger said that he would be great, and the Lord God would give him the throne of his father David; and he would reign over the house of Jacob forever. I was in shock. I said, 'How could this be, since I am a virgin?' The messenger said, 'The Holy Spirit will come upon you and the power of the most high will overshadow you, and for this reason the holy offspring shall be called the Son of God.'"

Mary looked at John, who read from the scroll, "'Therefore, the Lord himself will give you a sign: Behold, the virgin shall conceive and bear a son, and shall call his name Immanuel'" (Isaiah 7:14, NKJV).

John picked up the thread of the narrative.

"It gets even more specific. The child was to come from a specific family lineage. God promised Abraham that the seed would be from him. But the Scriptures go further yet and say that the seed would be from Abraham through Isaac and through Jacob. Abraham had two sons, but God eliminated Ishmael. Isaac had two sons, but God eliminated Esau. Jacob had twelve sons who became the twelve tribes of Israel, but God eliminated eleven and forecasted that the seed would come from the Tribe of Judah. God then gets specific regarding the family that produces the seed, which would be the family of Jesse, father to King David. Both Joseph and Mary are from the family of King David, but our culture only recognizes the heritage of the mother since…" John fumbled, and Mary smiled demurely.

"Since the father could be anybody," she supplied. Nodding, she said, "Naturally, Joseph knew the child was not his. But God sent a messenger to him to confirm what I had said and strengthen his confidence.

"Later a decree went out from Caesar Augustus that a census be taken. Everyone had to return to his city of origin to register. Joseph and I also went up from Galilee, from the city of Nazareth, to the city of David, which is Bethlehem. I gave birth in Bethlehem to my firstborn son and named him Jesus as the angel commanded."

John interjected, "Again, it was never their plan that Mary give birth in Bethlehem, but it had been recorded in Scripture. "'But you, Bethlehem Ephrathah, though you are little among the thousands of Judah, yet out of you shall come forth a ruler in Israel, whose going forth are from old, from everlasting' (Micah 5:2, NKJV).

How did the prophet Micah know that at that time Rome would conduct a census and send the whole world on a journey of relocation?"

With a faraway look in her eyes, Mary said, "Shepherds from the region appeared at the stable where we had placed my son in a manger. The inn was overcrowded, so they allowed us to stay in the stable. The shepherds told us that a multitude of angels appeared to them, praising God, and told them the Messiah was born and directed them to find us. And there were majestic wise men, which brought gifts for the baby."

"That, too, was foretold hundreds of years ago… " and John read from the scroll,

"'The kings of Tarshish and the isles with presents; the kings of Sheba and Seba will offer gifts'" (Psalm72: 10, NKJV).

"The visit of the kings drew attention, and Herod heard that a new king was born. Joseph was told in a dream to go to Egypt, and we stayed there until Herod was dead. We escaped the terrible tragedy, but so many others suffered." Mary bowed her head, and her voice broke.

John said, "Herod tried to find the child and have him executed. When he couldn't find him, he had all the children in the region under the age of two killed. It was predicted." John turned to the scroll in his hand and read, "'Thus says the Lord: "A voice was heard in Ramah, lamentations and bitter weeping, Rachel weeping for her children, refusing to be comforted for her children, because they are no more." (Jeremiah 31:15, NKJV).

Breathing deeply, Mary continued, "When we returned to the land of the Israelites, Joseph heard that Archelaus was reigning over Judea in place of his father, Herod. So we departed for the regions of Galilee and resided in the city called Nazareth." Mary smiled knowingly at the two soldiers. "Even I did not understand the depth or the immensity of who my son really is. It was not understood that the Messiah was to be God in the flesh. I had witnessed for the past three years wonders and miracles performed by his hands. And yet when he was arrested and crucified all the treasured memories seemed to disappear. After his burial all seemed lost."

Mary's face took on a glow, and she said, "Then he appeared to me and to these and to others. I now know and understand. He has risen, and that is the ultimate proof of who he is."

"We never understood this scripture until now," John said and rolled open another scroll. "'And I will put enmity between you and the woman and between your seed and her seed; He shall bruise your head, and you shall bruise his heel' (Genesis 3:15, NKJV). The meaning was a mystery until now. These words tell of a coming battle between the seed of the woman against the evil one. Her seed would be wounded as it crushed the head of the evil one. There are many ways we can interpret this passage. The only point I'm endeavoring to make is that someone was coming from the womb of a woman. If this Scripture stood alone it wouldn't mean much of anything.

But this Scripture along with literally hundreds of other predictions means everything. These Scriptures answer every important question about life that man can ask."

Marcus and Anthony were stunned by the revelations. For once, Anthony was speechless. He looked to Marcus for a response to the mysterious stories, but Marcus sat quietly. His face was a study of emotions, and Anthony was troubled by that. Marcus was a soldier, a man of action. He was a Roman, an educated man who did not indulge in fanciful thinking. Anthony wondered what Marcus was thinking now.

Anthony couldn't know that the Jewish stories had brought Marcus's wife back to him, as if she were sitting beside him. He could smell the fragrance of balsam—the ointment she used in washing her long, luxurious mane of silken brown hair. He could see the delicate bones of her tiny hands and feet. Her heartshaped face with the sharp planes of her high cheekbones, so sharp it seemed they could cut the papery thin skin that stretched across them. Everything about her was in miniature, except for her eyes. Her large, blue eyes, like liquid pools of feverish light, ringed with long, dark lashes.

Marcus' heart had gone into arrhythmia. He found it difficult to breathe, and he was horrified to think he might faint. He had adored his pretty little wife, and part of that love was for the religion he did not understand but which he respected, almost unwillingly. He had let her talk to him for hours about her people and their faith. It had been important to her. He knew that she had hoped he would convert to Judaism one day, but any esteem Marcus had held for the Jewish faith died when his wife died. Her God had let her die such a painful death. Recalling it now, Marcus literally could not breathe. He put his head down between his knees and found some relief. The others did not notice his agony because Peter was suddenly standing.

"Because of my cowardly behavior the night they arrested my Lord I have contempt for myself. But I realized something that I never realized before. There is no real strength in me. I am a man, a weak man."

Peter's voice was loud and brutish, but Marcus was listening. He was interested in what Peter had to say.

"So you think we may have stolen his body? We are Jews, and that is all we wish to be. His body being taken by us would bring us what? We would want to start another religion? And what would that bring us? No, it could only bring suffering for us and our children. Excommunication from our community. Ultimately, death for us all."

Peter paced the room, and then turned his tortured eyes on Marcus, who had lifted his head and was resting it on the edge of the table.

"The elders were accurate when they said the body is gone, but not by our hand. You yourself looked at me with contempt when we were introduced. And I deserved it. Yes, I am the supposed leader of this group, and I ran. Is that the type of person who would return to steal the body? How much more courage would my followers have than I? Did we not believe all was lost when they crucified Jesus? Did we not all run for our lives and abandon our Lord?"

The booming voice rose in pitch and crashed like a wave against a rock, and Peter wept uncontrollably.

Mary Magdalene grasped his meaty hands in her much smaller ones, but Peter shook his head and turned away. The group waited in uncomfortable silence for the big man to regain his composure.

When he did, he continued, his loud voice seeming all the stronger and emphatic.

"There is more evidence pointing to the resurrection of his body than the stealing of it. I witnessed his life for over three years, from the beginning of his ministry to his resurrection. He healed the sick. He gave sight to the blind. He raised the dead. He commanded the wind and calmed the storms. He gave us fish when there was no fish."

Peter pointed to the scroll before John. "Tell them, John."

And John read, "'I will raise up for them a Prophet like you from among their brethren, and will put my words in his mouth, and he shall speak to them all that I command'" (Deuteronomy 18:18, NKJV).

"Remember, John?" Peter said excitedly. "Remember about his anger in the temple?" And John read from another scroll, "'Because zeal for your house has eaten me up, and the reproaches of those who reproach you have fallen on me'" (Psalm 69:9, NKJV).

"And we cannot forget the witness in the wilderness, John the Baptist." Peter's voice was ringing now, echoing throughout the house.

John returned to the scroll of Isaiah.

"'A voice of one crying in the wilderness: "Prepare the way of the Lord; Make straight in the desert a highway for our God"'" (Isaiah 40:3, NKJV). Without waiting for any more prompting from Peter, John went on. "There are other Scriptures that speak of his ministry."

Then the eyes of the blind will be opened,
and the ears of the deaf will be unstopped.
Then the lame will leap like a deer, and the
tongue of the dumb will sing in joy.
Isaiah 35:5, 6 (NKJV)
And I will open my mouth in a parable; I
will utter dark sayings of old.
Psalm 78:2 (NKJV)

"Can you not see it is written that he would speak in parables?" pronounced Peter.

"Yes," responded John, "you are right. And a week before the crucifixion he entered Jerusalem on a donkey. Then the crowd cheered him, believing that he would bring in the kingdom promised in the Scriptures. They, like us, misunderstood. These events were also predicted.

"Zechariah wrote, 'Rejoice greatly, O daughter of Zion! Behold your King is coming to you; He is just and having salvation, humble, lowly and riding on a donkey, a colt, the foal of a donkey'" (Psalm 118:22, NKJV).

Peter interrupted excitedly, "Of all the prophesies the most significant are those that forecasted his resurrection. They made clear that his body, though it would be killed, would not see corruption. Here is one of many which were written almost a thousand years ago." And Peter read from the Psalms, "'For you will not leave my soul in Sheol; nor will you allow your holy one to see corruption'"

White-faced and breathing shallowly, Marcus, "That's a very interesting perspective from a man who committed treason against his so-called Lord. You speak as if you are filled with bravery, and yet when the circumstances are presented to you to prove your loyalty you cut and run. There is nothing you could say to me that I would consider creditable. You are a loud mouth with the backbone of a jellyfish. Even now you just stare at me. You should be offended to the point of rage. You should be willing now to defend your honor."

"Is that what makes a man? Your ability to assault with your tongue is weakness, not strength. Should we fear you because you can kill the body? You should fear the one who can kill both the body and the soul," cried Mary Magdalene.

Marcus glared at the woman. It was said she had been a prostitute, and Marcus suspected she still was. He did not believe a camp follower with loose morals would change so easily. What would be the point?

As if reading his mind, Mary Magdalene gazed at Marcus in genuine pity and disappointment. She spoke in a whisper, "I don't know what has really offended you." Moving closer to Marcus, she said, "Yes, I was worthy of nothing but contempt, but Jesus saw me otherwise. He knew that inwardly I wept for my sins. He forgave me, and that was the beginning of my new life. He loved me, and I loved him, but not as you would think. He loved me just as he loved the others, a love so great that he was willing to sacrifice himself. And I love him not as you would think, but as my Lord and God.

Know this…He appeared to me first at the tomb that Sunday morning. He appeared to Mary, Salome, and Joanna as they returned from the tomb that same morning. He has appeared to Simon Peter. And on that Sunday evening he appeared to ten of his disciples at Jerusalem. So reject it if you will, but that does not change the truth. Truth is truth whether you believe it or not."

Rising wearily to his feet, Marcus addressed Anthony as if the others were not present.

"I've heard enough for today. Let them know that they are not to leave the region for any reason. They will be interviewed again. If they cannot be found, they will be hunted down as fugitives. Also, retrieve all the names of the known disciples; we still have to make a point to interview them. I will get the horses and meet you outside. Make haste; I wish to make one more stop before we end the day."

As Anthony sprinted toward Marcus and the horses, he was perplexed to realize that he was ashamed of Marcus's behavior. Marcus could be hot-tempered and rash, but he was a professional. Today, though, he had acted like a novice. *I would like to question him*, Anthony thought, *but there has been enough humiliation today*

• • •

Riding at a cantor, Anthony ventured, "They were interesting interviews. What do you think about their story?"

When Marcus did not reply, Anthony became angry.

"I'm not your servant, and you don't intimidate me. If you've got a problem with this investigation, then you need to go home. Go find someone else you can humiliate. I'm sure there are plenty of people that will bow down to the great Centurion Marcus Flavius."

After several minutes, Marcus said, "Yes, they were interesting interviews."

Anthony waited, but Marcus said no more. The young man grabbed the harness of Marcus's horse and drew them both to a halt.

"If we are real partners, you are going to have to treat me as such. And if there is something on your mind and it pertains to this case or us, I have a right to know."

Marcus stared into the distance. He said, "There's no excuse for my behavior. I know better, and yet I let my anger get the better of me."

"What are you so angry about?"

Marcus stiffened his body and lifted his chin up in an attempt to get control of his emotions. "When Mary, the mother of Jesus, spoke she reminded me of my wife. My wife was a beautiful woman. She was of the Jewish faith, and she believed as these do that a great deliverer was coming—one like Moses of old, she would say. She really believed that, and she wanted me to believe it too."

Marcus paused, then continued, "Have you ever had someone you admired and loved die in your arms, Anthony?"

Anthony thought instantly of his son and fear gripped his heart, but he did not respond.

"It's not easy, especially when it's accompanied by great suffering. How one so pure could be made to suffer and the other one who desires death continue to live. During the last few days of her life I stayed by her side. I used every ounce of strength to keep my tears from flowing. But it seems I've become a weak, old man, like that Peter."

Marcus suddenly diverted his horse away from Anthony and went into a copse of trees.

Hidden deep in the cool darkness of the trees, Marcus threw himself prostrate on the grass and gave in to the shuddering sobs that racked his hardened body. He was not aware of the passage of time. He cried until the pain that ate at the center of his being subsided and retreated. He even dozed for a while. When he opened his eyes, he rolled over.

The branches connected overhead, forming a green canopy. *This is a holy place*, Marcus thought. *My very own temple.*

He was mocking himself, and yet there was a new sense of peace in his soul as he rose and returned to Anthony. The days of this investigation were having very strange effects on Marcus. He smiled to realize that he welcomed the strange effects. He had had enough of living with the pain.

Anthony, who had known he should leave his friend to his grief, had gotten off his horse and found a sun-warmed rock to rest upon. He was now lying on his rock bed blatantly snoring. Marcus laughed and tapped the young man gently with the toe of his boot. Anthony shook himself awake, and Marcus said, "There is a friend of mine who lives in the Greek quarter west of Jerusalem. We go back a long way. I respect his opinion, so I'm going to head over in that direction and attempt to catch up with him. I'm sure you're tired and want to return to your family. Don't feel obligated to come. I can catch up with you in the morning."

"You're not getting rid of me that easily. How far do we have to travel?"

"A few hours, but we can stop in the market for a bite to eat."

• • •

Back in the city, Marcus and Anthony stopped at an inn for food and drink. They had a little too much drink. Outside the inn, they fell asleep, using their horses' blankets for some comfort against the chilly night air. They woke up when they heard the city stirring back to life, just before dawn.

Heading along toward the Greek quarter, Marcus could see that Anthony had something on his mind. Anthony was a very transparent individual. He wore his emotions on his sleeve. Finally, Marcus said, "What?"

Sheepishly, Anthony responded, "What do you mean *what?* I didn't say anything. Do you want to say something? If you do, I'm listening."

"I'm saying this once. What is on your mind, Anthony?"

Anthony smiled. "If you insist. Do you think there is any validity to those testimonies? I mean, those prophecies were pretty specific. And those witnesses certainly believed what they were saying."

"Any reasonable person would have to consider those prophecies," Marcus responded. "They certainly didn't make them up. This is why I'm heading over to my friend and mentor Plato's residence. Among other things he is a great philosopher and engineer. He will always tell it like it is. I hold his opinion in high esteem."

Nervously, Anthony asked, "Do you believe in the gods?"

"That was the real question you had on your mind, wasn't it, Anthony?"

"Yes," Anthony shrugged, "it was."

"I'm glad you asked me. Now don't interrupt my answer. Do I believe in the gods? Hmmm. Let's see, where do I begin? Do you mean the god Adrammeleh, a Babylonian god worshiped by the Sepharvites? Or Asherah, the wife of Baal, a Canaanite god? Or Ashima, a Hittite god worshipped by the people of Hamath? Or Ashtoreththe, the Syrian and Phoenician goddess of the moon, sexual love, and fertility?

Or Baal, the chief male deity of the Phoenicians and Canaanites? How about Chemosh, the national god of the Moabites and Ammonites? Or Dianna? I'm sure you're familiar with this Roman goddess of the moon, hunting, wild animals, and virginity. What about Hermes the Greek god of commerce, science, invention, cunning? Or the great Zeus, the supreme god of Greeks?"

"*All right!*" Anthony shouted. "I get your point. If you want to mock my question rather than answer in a mature, intelligent way, that's fine with me. I will not ask you your opinion again."

Marcus laughed a full, round belly laugh. He felt so good this morning. He said, "I'm sorry. I was just attempting to make a point. Your question is a valid one. I'm not sure what I believe. It seems to me when one studies the different religions that they all have one thing in common. They all seem to make their gods in man's image. And in most cases these gods reflect the worst in man's nature. They are violent or perverted. These gods manipulate the people. And the priests use them to keep the masses in check. And these gods can't seem to answer some of the most important questions, like why does this or that happen? Or why does he or she suffer? Or why are we here?"

"I appreciate your honesty," said Anthony, "but I have another view. I don't know much about all the past civilizations and their gods, but I do know that every civilization from past to present believed in some type of god or gods. I find that intriguing. It seems to me that there is something deep within the heart of all men that consciously or unconsciously declares this idea that there is one who is much greater than us.

I realize what you said, that we make gods up in our minds and in our own image to control and manipulate. But that still does not answer why we have this innate idea of a greater power. The mere fact that we question says something about the possibility. We don't understand something, so we say it must be the gods. But what makes us come up with that? Where does that idea come from? The idea of God? Could it not be that there is a God or gods?"

Marcus smiled and shook his head. "You are going to get along well with Plato. He lives for these types of conversations."

With a Philosopher

Marcus and Anthony approached a medium- size brown stucco home. Fountains and statues lined the pathway leading to the entrance. After tying the horses' reins to the low-hanging branches of nearby trees, they walked up the path.

Suddenly the door swung open with a shout.

"Is it really you?"

Marcus was enveloped in a fierce bear hug by a full-bearded man whose leathery brown skin was as lined and wrinkled as a walnut shell.

"It has been too long. At least seven years." The old man took a step back and scrutinized Marcus. "I've missed you. Where have you been?"

Before Marcus could answer, the old man said, "Where are my manners? Come in, come into my home."

They walked into the house and followed the old man, who did not cease talking.

"What brings you here? Is there something you need? Oh, I must calm down, but I can't. Marcus, I'm so excited to see you. This visit brings me much joy. I have missed your company very much. You are staying! I won't take no for an answer. Please stay, stay a few days. We will catch up. There's much to talk about."

Smiling, Marcus said, "My good and faithful friend, it has been too long. I've missed your friendship and counsel."

Turning toward Anthony, Marcus said, "Plato, this is Anthony."

The old man peered intently at the much younger man, dressed in the uniform of a Roman soldier. He took in the tousled blond curls, laughing blue eyes, and mischievous grin.

Plato nodded his head, and when Anthony extended his hand, he clasped it between both of his. Warmly, he said, "My boy." Plato gestured. "Come, come and sit. Let us sit and drink and talk. This is a special day. You have made this a special day."

After the wine was poured and the men had raised their goblets in a toast to friends, old and new, Plato turned to Marcus and said, "What? What is the matter? I see that you are troubled. What is it? What can I do?"

Marcus looked at Anthony and smiled. "See? What did I tell you? He doesn't miss a trick. I was never able to get anything by him. He sees right through me."

Anthony could see that the fondness and special bond between Marcus and Plato went back a long time. They were friends, but they also seemed like father and son. The two men beamed at each other with genuine joy on their faces, and Marcus was relaxed in Plato's presence as Anthony had never observed in his mentor before. Marcus's defenses were down; he felt safe with Plato.

To Plato, Marcus answered, "Yes, I do have a problem. Actually, it's more of a mystery. I'm having a problem coming up with answers. Or maybe I'm looking for answers that suit my view. I have a dilemma, and I've come for your advice."

"You have come to the right place!" Plato shouted with delight. "You know us Greeks, we love to question. You know, Marcus, the greatest and wisest men ever to walk the earth were Plato and Socrates. I am named after one of them." Plato smiled. "They always questioned and sought answers. They questioned what truth was and what goodness meant. They endeavored to explain what justice is. Their queries often made people angry, but they didn't care. They wanted people to look for truth and not accept any substitution. Socrates believed that the wisest people were those who admitted they knew very little. So, let us relax and enjoy one another's company. Then we will answer your question and solve your problem."

"Eternally optimistic. I've missed that," said Marcus.

While Plato busied himself at the hearth, concocting one of his special meals, the three men entertained one another with their adventures and exploits of the last several years. Eventually, Plato brought to the table an assortment of grilled vegetables, cakes made of chickpeas, and brown bread.

As they ate, Anthony admired the statues that lined the outside pathway and the interior hallways.

"Did you sculpt them?" he asked.

"Yes, I did, Anthony, and I have many more in my workshop. My friend Hermenous is supposed to stop by today. We have been working on some interesting experiments and inventions. I'm sure you will like him. He's a bit peculiar. He's not one for cleanliness. His hair could use a trim. His beard reaches his waist," laughed Plato. "So what's the difference? He's of good character, not to mention a genius and a great mathematician. His tricks will impress you. He has created some mechanical machines, which are in my workshop. I will demonstrate them to you later, after you are refreshed."

Finally, they finished their meal, and Plato addressed the anxiety he had noted on Marcus's face.

"So then, explain to me this great mystery. I am excited to consider your problem."

Marcus and Anthony took turns explaining to Plato all that they had uncovered in the investigation concerning the missing body of Jesus and the evidence at the scene of the crime. When one man skipped a portion or inadvertently left out a detail, the other man filled it in. Anthony showed Plato the sketch he had made of the tomb.

When the soldiers had completed their review, Plato looked puzzled. His brow was furrowed in a frown, and he asked, "You are having a problem recovering the body; is what disturbs you…or is there something else?"

Marcus stared into Plato's eyes like a devoted pupil.

"Yes, it's much more than that. We have a situation that seems to be unraveling. It's as if an avalanche has begun, and we are in its path. I have never dealt with such a unique set of circumstances. Even the suspects are different than the usual. They are not criminals nor do I believe they are even capable of criminal intent." Afraid of sounding maudlin, Marcus said with some embarrassment, "I hate to bother you with this problem…"

Forcefully, Plato interrupted, "Don't ever speak like that. There's nothing you could ever do that would be a bother to me. Just take your time and explain to me the situation. I will do everything in my power to assist you. There is an answer for every question under the sun. Some questions are more difficult than others, but we will search and find the answers."

Humbly, Marcus said, "Thank you. I have always appreciated your concern and friendship. Your confidence inspires me."

Anthony was amazed by the interaction between Plato and Marcus. He had never seen Marcus so open and unguarded.

Plato looked thoughtful. "I have heard of this Jew named Jesus."

"Please, tell us what you have heard concerning this Jesus. Apparently he has made an indelible impact on many people, and I really want to hear what you know about him and his life."

Nodding his head, Plato responded, "I don't have any direct knowledge, but I have heard many things. There is a certain centurion who lives less than a mile from here who did have direct contact with him. It is reported that this Jesus healed someone in his household. I myself cannot confirm that, but you might want to check his story out.

"In any event, the word around here concerning his life comes mostly from the Jewish population. I've heard them speak of him as their messiah, sent from God to free them from the bondage of Rome. He apparently made these assertions about himself. Of course that wouldn't be the first time I've heard such a story. It seems the Jews have been hopeful of a great deliverer for a long time." Plato's frown deepened, and he said, "There was talk of his supernatural powers. People say he healed leprosy and fed thousands with a few baskets of food. There is one story that he healed a man blind from birth by spitting on dirt and placing the dirt in the blind man's eyes."

Plato smiled, not derisively, and continued, "Some people called him a great prophet, others called him a king. I know that people flocked from all over the region to hear him speak. I often saw the great crowds. It is reported that he spoke in parables, stories. Because of that, there was much discussion and heated debate about the meaning of his words. Yet, in spite of the controversy, people were in awe of his words, which pierced the heart and seemed to come directly from heaven, they say. I would have gone to see him myself, but I've been consumed with my theories and experiments."

Plato was silent a moment before continuing.

"There is another side to the coin, however. He apparently had many confrontations with the temple leaders. It was reported that the priests of the temple were out to get him. They alleged that he committed blasphemy against their God. They asserted that he forgave people of their sins, and only God is capable of such an act. When I heard that the priests finally got their way and convinced the Roman authorities that he was a threat to the empire, I felt very depressed. Human nature has not changed."

Taking a deep breath, Marcus said, "We have this list of unsettling details and intriguing events, but… " Marcus looked directly into Plato's eyes to emphasize the importance of what he was about to say. "But," he repeated, "it appears that these events were foretold hundreds of years ago. Not only that, but after interviewing several of his followers, including his mother, it appears that his birth, his life, and his death were all prophesied. Throughout their Jewish book it speaks of him, from his lineage to the works he would do and the very words that he would speak. We saw it for ourselves as we examined their scrolls with some of his followers. I'm having a real problem making sense of these things. This should be a simple investigation, culminating in the recovery of a corpse. Instead, it has turned into something quite different. I'm not even sure how to categorize it. *Who is this Jesus?*"

Looking eagerly at Plato in expectation of an answer, Marcus said, "According to the testimony of these witnesses, Jesus of Nazareth claimed to be the Son of God, who was predestined to die on a cross for the sins of the world, and who rose from the dead on the third day to prove his claim. *What am I to think?*"

Plato marveled at what he had heard. Getting to his feet, he paced around the room while he contemplated Marcus's information. Finally, he asked, "Have you considered a different direction in your investigation?"

Confused, Marcus questioned, "What do you mean? What other direction is there than to pursue witnesses in order to reveal the facts? All investigations attempt to answer the questions of who, what, when, where, how, and why. We know what happened, when it happened, where it happened, how it happened, and who it happened to and why they did it. We just don't know where the body is now. I'm not following your logic. What exactly do you mean by a *different direction* in this investigation?"

"I would suggest that there is one question you have not answered satisfactorily. In fact, you may not have seriously considered this question. There is a more important question than where the body is. I believe if you seek to answer the more important question, you will find the body."

Marcus sighed. "Plato, don't do this to me. Do not speak in riddles."

"I'm sorry, Marcus, I don't wish to frustrate you. The question you want answered is not where the body is, but who is this person? You see, my son, if what you are discovering in your investigation is fact concerning this Jesus, then where the body is may only be answered by answering the question of who he is. That is the most important question to be answered. You may have already answered that question, you just don't realize it."

Marcus appeared frustrated, and Plato pleaded, "Let me finish. It will make sense after I give you my full perspective on these events. First, let me begin with the empty tomb. Logic dictates only two explanations. One, Jesus was removed from the tomb by his enemies or by his friends. If by his enemies, what would be their motive? If they removed the body, would they not enthusiastically produce it in order to negate his assertion of being the Son of God and having the power to arise from the dead? Therefore, they have no motive and must be eliminated as the thieves. What of his friends? Did you not tell me earlier that they abandoned him? So then they lacked the courage to attempt such an act.

"This leads me to the second possibility. This event is not a human work, but a divine work. I would encourage you to consider deeply the evidence you have already uncovered concerning the life of Jesus. Let us consider some of these things together. I believe that we can deduce the answers in a logical manner. But know this, the answer may be extremely startling and have implications beyond your investigation."

Marcus and Anthony were excited by Plato's comments. They knew the events were unique, and they were having trouble interpreting the meaning of these events. The fact that Plato was so confident in his ability to come to a logical explanation kept them at ease. The two soldiers realized that this was the reason they had come to this aged man. They hunched forward and awaited Plato's analyses.

"Let us consider what your investigation uncovered concerning what was said about him, and what he said about himself. I believe by answering these questions we can discover the answer to who Jesus is, man or God. Tell me, what have you concluded regarding the character of Jesus?"

Anthony answered, "To me, it appears that if nothing else he was a good man. Everything we have uncovered points to the fact that he was a decent and caring person. Even if he did not perform the wonders and miracles that have been attributed to him, he still treated people with dignity."

Plato nodded his head, and even Marcus found himself agreeing with his partner. "Very good, Anthony," said Plato. "Now, let me ask you this, what did Jesus say about himself? What has your investigation uncovered?"

"According to the temple priests he committed blasphemy, and that's why they wanted him put to death. He said he was the Son of God. He claimed he could forgive sins. From some of the testimony of our soldiers who were at the crucifixion, Jesus spoke as if he were from another place, another world or, as he called it, another kingdom. He even went so far as promising this thief that was hanging on a cross next to him that he was going to be with him in a place called Paradise."

"Excellent observations, Anthony. What about you, Marcus, what have you concluded thus far?"

"Well, you've heard the testimony." Marcus waved his hand loosely. "Some of these predictions…"

"That's not what I mean," Plato interrupted. "My question is, what you have concluded through your investigation, specifically your interviews, concerning Jesus' character? What do you think of him, and what did he think of himself?"

Marcus swallowed. "No one was able to pinpoint any evil or criminal act. According to testimony, even the testimony of Pilate, he demonstrated perfect forbearance. Except for the temple leaders, whom Pilate determined to be false witnesses, everyone has had positive comments concerning his character. As far as what he thought of himself, he said he was not of this world." Marcus looked at Plato almost in anger. "Plato, I am becoming frustrated by your line of questioning. Please, get to the point."

"Yes, Marcus, I will now get to the point. Hopefully, you will think it was worth your wait. There are only three possibilities concerning this Jesus. It is clear from what his followers stated that he considered himself the Messiah. He taught that he was the Son of God, preaching the kingdom of God. Furthermore, as you investigated the disappearance of the body, you interviewed witnesses and concluded by their testimony that he was a good man. Even when he appeared before the governor, Pilate could find no fault in him. When you spoke to those closest to him, they described him as a man of God. If anyone could point out Jesus' faults it would be those closest to him. And yet there is no accusation. Even in the worst of circumstances, being crucified, your own guards could not point out any fault. Jesus actually forgave them for their actions!"

Plato's voice rose as he stressed the extraordinariness of Jesus. "So then, he must have been a good man. But I say *no*. I say *not at all*. How could he be a good man? Did he not say he was the Son of God? Sent by God? If that is not the absolute truth, then he is a liar."

Marcus felt his jaw tighten as he considered Plato's statements. But the old man wasn't finished.

"What else could he be? Does one who is good say that he is a messiah? Could a person be a good person and say that he has the power to forgive sins if it were not true? According to everything you have told me regarding his own view of himself, how could he be good if what he said is not true? One would have to conclude that this Jesus was one of the world's greatest liars. He lied about himself and convinced many to follow this lie.

"Consider his impact. He apparently convinced the closest people to him that he was more than a man. Is this a lie? If it is, he is in no way a good and decent man.

"Now, if it is a lie, one must ask how this lie benefited him. Liars have a motive. They lie to benefit themselves. How would this lie benefit Jesus? Answer: it wouldn't. In fact, rather than benefiting him, it became the reason to execute him. Pilate gave him ample opportunity to recant his alleged statements concerning himself, but he did not. That benefited him *how*?"

Looking intently at Marcus and Anthony, Plato said, "Take a moment and consider what I'm saying. Jesus said many things concerning who he was. What he said is either true or false. If it is false, then he cannot be considered a good man; he must be considered a liar. That's a logical conclusion. Reason dictates that if a man is a liar and manipulates people into believing a lie, he cannot be a good man." Plato paused. "Are you following my argument?"

"I'm not sure," Marcus said.

Staring at Marcus and then turning to Plato, Anthony smiled and said, "You made the point that if Jesus were a liar he could not be a good man. That I understand. However, I don't understand where you're going with this argument."

Plato smiled. "You will. Jesus was not a good man if, in fact, he was a liar. So then, is there another alternative?" Answering his own question, Plato said, "Yes, I believe so. If he was not lying, he must have been a madman."

Marcus and Anthony burst into laughter. More than once, Marcus had considered this possibility.

Plato smiled and said, "Let's examine this theory. Clearly there are people who are madmen, not in their right minds. They are not responsible for their actions. There is no evil intent in what they say or do. They cannot help themselves. They see themselves from a totally preposterous perspective. If this Jesus was not a liar, then we must conclude that he was a lunatic."

Looking at Anthony, Plato continued, "If you believed you were the greatest warrior that ever lived, I would say that you were quite arrogant. If you argued that you were Alexander the Great, I would argue that something was loose upstairs. If you said you were a tiger, I would conclude that you were a lunatic. And if you said that you were God, you would be as crazy as they come. Pure and simple, you must be a madman. So then, according to your investigation, we must conclude that Jesus was as crazy as they come because he said he was God.

"Yet, we must consider his assertions in the context of his life. Jesus had qualities that liars and lunatics lack. He demonstrated prudence, wisdom in practical affairs, according to your investigation. He was known for his compassion and forgiving heart. He was capable of empathizing with people and did so throughout his ministry. When teaching, he was able to connect the dots so that those who heard would understand his theology and philosophical views. This is not a description of a man who is a lunatic. Putting together all the evidence, witnesses, predictions, his ministry, and the missing body, a reasonable person would have to conclude that this Jesus was not, nor could have been, a liar or a lunatic. Therefore, I must conclude through the argument of logic that he was who he said he was. The Son of God."

The three men exchanged meaningful looks.

"I realize this is a startling statement," said Plato, "And, of course, this would bring us to another question. If God were capable of becoming human, what kind of human would he be? However, I believe there is a more important question. Why would God become a man?"

Marcus held up both hands. "*Stop*! That's all we can handle. This is too much to take in."

Anthony concurred. "My head is spinning. I need to rest."

Nodding and smiling, Plato said, "These assertions are difficult. Take the time to consider them. You both are tired. I want you to spend the night. I insist. Tomorrow you can continue on your quest. I implore you to consider my arguments. There may not be a human answer to the missing body."

Plato suddenly looked perturbed. "I was expecting Hermenous tonight. He must have been delayed or distracted by something else. I really want you to meet him. He has tremendous insight. Come, I will show you to your rooms."

• • •

As the men walked down the corridor, Plato slapped his forehead and said, "Oh! I almost forgot! Before you leave, I want to show you my workshop." Grinning, he said, "I'm sure you will be impressed."

Recalling their earlier conversation, Plato added, "That centurion I told you about lives less than a mile from here. I suggest you interview him. He is one of your own, and I'm sure you will uncover a very interesting perspective."

"Thank you, Plato," Marcus said. "We will stop by the centurion's house, and then report back to Pilate. We still need to interview those guards that were assigned to the tomb. They have been on assignment in Joppa. Maybe they are back at the garrison."

In their separate rooms, both Anthony and Marcus passed a restless night.

Marcus pondered all the evidence and testimony they had uncovered.

How in the world can this be true? There are tens of thousands of opinions and belief systems. Who's to say what's right? How is it that the greatest minds never grasped… Everything that I have ever been taught has to be reconsidered in light of this investigation.

Marcus smiled as he considered the real possibility that his beloved wife actually understood these things.

Just as the sky was beginning to lighten, heralding the dawn, Marcus rubbed his eyes and was startled as two blurred faces came into view before his strained eyes.

Marcus rose with a shout, "What in the name…

Plato, what is going on? Are you crazy? What is your face doing in mine? And who is this?"

"Good morning, Marcus. This is my friend, Hermenous. He finally arrived. I spent the whole night explaining to him all about your investigation. He is absolutely enthralled by what you have uncovered. I also prepared a hearty breakfast. Come, let us eat and talk.

"By the way, Anthony is dressing. We woke him up earlier. He appears a bit ill-tempered."

"I'm sure he is. Did you wake him up the same way you woke me? Get out; let me get dressed in peace. I'll meet you at the table in a moment."

Anthony was already seated when Marcus arrived for breakfast, and Plato and Hermenous followed him into the room, bearing platters of succulent food.

"Good morning, Marcus," said Anthony. "Were you woken by these two lovely birds this morning?"

The four men looked at each other and began to laugh.

As they enjoyed the meal, they discoursed on the investigation. Hermenous seemed mesmerized by what he called the possibilities, although the soldiers found his conversation difficult to follow. He mumbled when he spoke, and it was difficult to understand him when he talked in mathematical terms. Throughout the discussion, Hermenous used a writing tablet on which he scribbled calculations.

"Did you consider my argument during the night?" Plato asked Anthony and Marcus.

"I promise that I will consider everything you have said. I hold your opinion in high regard. But I didn't have the strength to think about it last night, though my sleep was disturbed by the possibilities." Rising to his feet, Marcus said, "Plato, we must take our leave. We have much to accomplish and little time to do it. Pilate is very demanding, and we must complete this investigation one way or the other."

"Would you do me one favor? It will only take a few minutes," responded Plato.

"Anything," Marcus replied. "What do you wish?"

"To be honest, the one favor is actually two requests," the old man said and smiled.

Shaking his head, Marcus returned the smile. "Of course, you would not have one simple request."

"I would like you and Anthony to come into my workshop. I would like your opinion on something. And afterward I would like you to consider something that Hermenous worked up. Would you do that?"

They all proceeded to Plato's workshop. His workshop resembled the library of Joseph of Arimathea, the walls lined with scrolls. Manuscripts from centuries past lay on nearby tables. Unlike Joseph's library, the workshop also contained pulley systems and mechanical machines that seemed to be moving on their own power, much to the astonishment of the soldiers.

"What in the world have you been up to?" Marcus's eyes fell upon what appeared to be a geometrical diagram.

Plato noticed Marcus's interest in the design.

"That is the Pythagorean theorem. This formula states that the square of a right triangle's hypotenuse equals the sum of the squared lengths of the two remaining sides."

Marcus smirked and said with his usual hint of sarcasm, "No doubt, but I'm not admiring that document. What I am amazed at is this machine. It looks like it's moving on its own."

"Oh, yes, one of my greatest inventions." Plato pointed to a wall behind the machine. "This is where the power comes from. When I heat this water, it turns into steam. When the steam builds enough pressure, it pushes on the top of this lid, which releases the steam into the cylinder, which then fires this arrow into this wooden target. It is amazing that a little bit of pressure from the steam gives the arrow tremendous thrust. I believe with a little more research we will be able to make a weapon that will thrust an arrow or projectile a great distance."

Beckoning Marcus, Plato said, "Marcus, come closer and marvel at what Aristarchus proposed. And I agree with his theory. Aristarchus proposed that the earth and other planets revolve around the sun. Other astronomers disagree; however, I find it intriguing."

Presenting Marcus a diagram of the planetary theory, Plato continued, "See how the sun is in the center, and the other planets revolve around it? And look here; see how Hipparchus figured out how to map the sky? He invented the grid system. He called it longitude and latitude. It gives us the ability to map out exact positions of the stars. Now, Marcus, I would like you to sit here on this chair. Anthony, you can stand with me and Hermenous and observe. Marcus, look around and tell me what you see. Take your time and observe everything that is in this room."

"Why do you have to make everything so dramatic?

Can't you just tell me what it is I'm supposed to see?" Anthony found himself suppressing laughter at the petulant whine he detected in Marcus's voice.

"Please, Marcus, humor me," replied the old man.

Marcus gazed around the perimeter of the room. He noticed many things he had not noticed before. There were statues of animals, such as lions, elephants, and horses, in various stages of sculpting. In a cage in the corner was a beautiful yellow and black bird that Marcus was surprised to discover he had earlier overlooked.

After several minutes of contemplation, Marcus was exasperated.

"Plato, did I not explain earlier that I have lots to accomplish? I'm not sure what you're looking for, but I've just about had enough."

Plato barked back, "Marcus, what do you see?"

Marcus exclaimed, "I see genius all around this room! Everything I observe screams of your genius and intellect. I marvel at your abilities to draw and create machines that are so wonderfully made. I am proud to know such an intellectual and creative spirit. But even more astonishing is with all your abilities you have managed to stay humble."

Plato jumped like an excited child. He shouted, "I knew you would come to the correct conclusion! I'm not sure whether you actually understand the implications of your observations, but I will explain them. And I believe if you consider my explanation in conjunction with my other theories concerning your investigation, you may come to a concrete conclusion based on what is true.

"What you have described is called empirical evidence. You studied what is here in this room and concluded that behind the creative work is a mind. You concluded without much thought that the items in this room, in and of themselves, dictate an intelligent being, someone who has the ability and the intelligence and the energy to put these things together. If you questioned anyone in their right mind concerning these issues they would have to arrive at the same conclusion."

Turning to the bird in the corner, Plato said, "Now what about the bird? I'm sure you realize that I did not make this beautiful creature that has the natural ability to fly. When I consider the makeup of this bird I marvel. Within its nature it feeds itself, makes a nest for its young, and cares for them until they are able to care for themselves. And, of course, we can say the same regarding the animal kingdom at large." Waving his hands in the air, Plato went on, "The birds that migrate. The wolves that work together like soldiers, strategizing their predatory moves. The lioness that protects her cubs with her life. We call this *animal instinct*. However, that is a facade. The fact is we lack a real answer for why creatures act the way they do. What we call animal instinct is really nothing more than our admittance that we don't know why they do what they do." Plato giggled like a madman. "I love the terminology; *survival instinct*...what a cover-up for a lack of an answer.

"Now what of *us*? Marcus, if you had would demonstrate through logic legitimate arguments regarding the real probability of intelligence behind the designs of this world, but I know that your time is limited. Therefore, I will ask you to consider the possibility that there cannot be design without a designer. There cannot be mathematics without a mathematician.

"There is no empirical evidence of anything being organized without a mind behind it. There are great inventions and great mathematicians, but the formulas they deduce are already present. They just happened to identify them as such. You will have to consider all that I have said in light of your investigation. Now, you promised me two requests. Is that correct?"

Marcus sighed. "Yes, yes, yes. But this must not take more than a moment."

"Thank you," said Plato. Turning to Hermenous, Plato's voice betrayed his delighted anticipation. "Her- menous, please show Marcus and Anthony your calculations. Earlier this morning, before you and Anthony awoke, I laid out to Hermenous all the facts concerning your investigation. I know I told you that earlier. However, what I didn't tell you was that Hermenous did a mathematical analysis, which is based upon principles of probability. And he…Well, I'll let him tell you."

"Thank you, my esteemed colleague. First, I would like to—"

"Get to the point," Plato said hastily. "Marcus is ready to leave."

Marcus and Anthony laughed out loud.

"Of course," said Hermenous, "What I did was calculate the probability of anyone from the past to the present being able to fulfill just eight of the prophecies that I reviewed last night. For example, Jesus' place of birth, time of birth, manner of birth, being betrayed the way he was, manner of death, people's reaction, such as mocking, spitting, staring. His being pierced without a broken bone, and his burial in a tomb of a rich man. These were all the predictions that Plato described to me last night and early this morning before you woke up. What I'm about to say may be difficult to comprehend. I don't mean that you are not intelligent or capable of understanding, no, not at all. What I mean is the probability of these events occurring by chance is astronomically incomprehensible."

Observing the vacant looks on the soldiers' faces, Hermenous sighed.

"Let me try to explain. If you know anything about mathematics, you know that a number can be given a power, which allows the number to be multiplied by the powered number. Simply put, ten times ten gives you 100. If you have ten to the third power that would mean ten times ten times ten, and that would give you 1,000. Now, if you have ten to the fifth power, that would mean you would have ten times ten times ten times ten times ten, and that would give you the number 100,000. Am I making myself clear?"

Appearing bewildered, Marcus said, "I understand. It's not a difficult equation."

Hermenous nodded. "Good. Now, I'll get to my point. For these events to occur by chance the probabilities are ten to the seventeenth power. That means one chance in…" Hermenous wrote on his writing tablet 1,000,000,000,000,000,000. He was gratified by the look of awe that came over the solders' faces now. "Unbelievable, isn't it? We don't have a name for that number."

There were few moments of silence while the men considered Hermenous's revelations. Then he spoke again.

"I would like to show you another formula, but you probably would have trouble understanding. In order for you to comprehend the very limited possibility of these events occurring by chance, I will illustrate it by a literal example. If we took enough silver coins and laid them on the surface of the land of Judea, and have the coins cover all of Judea two feet deep, and then mark one of these silver coins so as to be able to identify it as such, and stir the whole mass thoroughly, all over the land…then we have a blind man travel as far as he wishes, but he must pick up the one silver coin and it must be the *right one*! What chance would he have of getting the right one? Just the same chance that these Jewish prophets would have had of writing these eight prophecies and having them all come true in one man."

With a flourish, Plato shouted, "So then, one must deduce that these prophecies either came about by chance or some intelligent mind was behind the writings!"

Clasping his hands behind his back and walking about the room, Marcus said, "These are some astonishing assertions. I promise you that we will consider your perspectives and insights. But for now, before you exhaust me any further, we will take our leave. I promise you that we will stop and see that centurion you mentioned earlier. Hopefully, we will bring this investigation to a conclusion." Suddenly reconsidering his last remark, Marcus said vehemently, *"No, it will get done!"*

• • •

At the roadside, Plato and Hermenous embraced Anthony and Marcus and bid them farewell. Plato reminded Marcus to return after the completion of the investigation. The old man was very curious as to the final outcome. With his eyes twinkling, Plato said, "I think you will uncover more than a missing body with this investigation!"

Marcus and Anthony rode in the direction of the centurion's house without speaking. Finally, Anthony asked what he always asked.

"So, what do you think?"

Marcus was grim when he answered.

"I don't know what to think. Those two wise men have nothing to gain by giving an opinion one way or the other. Unlike everyone else we have interviewed so far."

The men continued in silence for several paces. Then Marcus spoke again.

"In any event all these conjectures must be considered. Plato elaborated on a great point in a very logical manner. His mind works in such an analytical way. Who could have come up with such a viewpoint? That Jesus is either a liar or a lunatic or the Lord. That logic is absolutely reasonable."

Anthony stared at his mentor.

"You know, there is many a night when I have stood gazing at the stars, and I couldn't help but feel so insignificant. The vastness of the night sky makes me feel so small. And there are times when I question the reality of a god. But when Plato took us into his workshop and questioned you on what you observed, that made sense to me. I think about our roads and buildings and aqueducts, and it is self-evident to me that there is power, energy, and intelligence behind these creations. How much more of a mind when one looks at the natural world? Did you ever watch an ant colony work or a flower blossom? It just makes sense; at least to my way of thinking. The grass, the flowers, the insects and animals did not invent themselves. I can't think of anything that is organized that does not have an intellect behind it."

"Yes, Anthony, but there are still plenty of questions that I would need answered before I bought into any of these suppositions. And, frankly, I'm not in the mood to discuss these issues. Let's concentrate on the other witnesses we need to interview."

Realizing that Marcus was through with the conversation, Anthony said no more. Inwardly, he knew he was moving toward the very real possibility that this investigation may have worldwide significance. He thought, *How in the world I could be involved in something with such magnitude is beyond me. Could it really be possible for a mere human to actually know God?*

The Faith

The friendship between Marcus's family and Plato's family went back several generations. The enmity and even the war for empire, which occurred between the two dominant world powers, had not affected that friendship. As a child, Marcus had been a student of Plato in Greece.

The two men found themselves today in the same desert region of Judea for widely differing reasons, yet the reasons were connected. Plato was intrigued by the Hebrew faith in one God and by the promises and prophecies put forth in their book. Living among the Jews had always been his desire and destiny. It was part scientific experiment, part the hungering search of the soul for concrete answers to abstract questions.

Marcus was dispatched to the arid land under Roman rule as a soldier of his country. But his childhood spent under the tutelage of Plato, and the history of the Hebrew people, had prepared him for the special work he was often called upon to perform for Rome. He had an understanding of these mysterious people as a result of his boyhood lessons with the philosopher. Certainly, his marriage had added to that understanding.

Lost in his thoughts beside Anthony, as they made their way to the centurion's house, Marcus was far away. He was a child again in Greece, and Plato's dark skin was still smooth. The teacher was speaking to the young boys seated at his feet. Marcus remembered Plato's exact words.

"We study history, such as prior war tactics, to assist us in determining the mindset of a people. Knowing how far they will go for their beliefs is important. A people such as the Spartans of old who are schooled in the concept of glorification for those who die in battle, makes them a formidable foe. On the other hand, a self-centered people can easily be divided and conquered. In the case of the Hebrews, they have been formidable at different times in history. But now they are a divided and subdued people. Yet there are some splinter groups that a ruling government has to be concerned with."

Marcus liked the discussion of wars and world conquest, so he rolled his eyes when another student raised his hand and said, "I would like to understand more fully the belief system of the Jews. They seem to have a unique belief system."

Plato appeared pleased with the request and replied, "Ah, but it's a long story." Marcus was not the only one who groaned loudly.

Plato laughed. "My boys, stories are always better told with a little action." While Plato went to the closet for his puppets, Marcus joined the others in pummeling the questioner. When Plato turned back to the class, the boys were sitting in their places, backs rigid and eyes ahead.

"Most of what we know about the early history of the Hebrews is contained in the first five books of their sacred text. These writings describe some events that actually happened. We know this because there are other written sources that tell us about the same subjects. Therefore, we will accept the Hebrew version of history when it coincides with other sources.

"However, their book speaks of them as a special people and their god as the only god. Their book also tells of great supernatural events. Let me start from the beginning. According to their book, their god chose a man named Abraham to be the father, or first, of the Hebrew people," and Plato held aloft one of his puppets. The boys understood the puppet to represent Abraham, father of the Hebrews.

"Abraham was a shepherd and lived in Ur, in Mesopotamia. God commanded him to move his people and their flocks to Palestine, which was called Canaan back then. Abraham promised God that he and his people would always obey him. God, in turn, promised to always protect them from their enemies. This was the first of many covenants, or promises, between their god and the Hebrews. Abraham begat Isaac, and Isaac, Jacob." Again, Plato held aloft the various Hebrew representatives. "Jacob had twelve sons who later grew into the twelve tribes. They were in Canaan for a while, and their crops failed. They moved south into Egypt, and over time they were forced to become slaves. Eventually, a man named Moses led them out of Egypt. Moses supposedly performed signs and wonders. There's one story of him ordering the Hebrews to sacrifice a lamb and paint the blood over their door posts. An angel of death moved over the land, and all those without the blood on the posts lost their firstborn sons. The Egyptians did not have the blood on their doorposts, and all families lost their firstborn. At that point, Pharaoh let them go."

Plato's puppets were moving wildly about in the air as he made them enact the tale. Plato smiled.

"The Hebrews disobeyed their god on the way back to Canaan and were forced to wander in the wilderness for forty years. After Moses died, the Hebrews finally reached Palestine and settled. They were organized into twelve tribes. Each tribe was separate from the others. But in times of danger they would unite under leaders called Judges. They had other leaders called Prophets. These prophets said that they were messengers sent by God to tell the people how he wanted them to act. These prophets told the people that they had two duties…to worship God and to deal in just and fair ways with one another. Not a bad philosophy for life," and Plato was gratified by the nodding heads of his students.

Apparently undaunted by the pummeling, the questioning student, named Damokles, raised his hand again to inquire, "So these twelve tribes are the Jews of today?"

"No," Plato replied, "but that is an excellent question."

Damokles looked smugly at his classmates.

Plato continued, "After the Hebrews settled in the south central part of Palestine, they expanded south and north. They fought with their neighbors at different times and for various reasons. They had some great warriors; at least that's what is recorded. Around nine hundred years ago, their greatest king, named David, had a son who also became king. His name was Solomon. This Solomon was the most powerful of the Hebrew kings. He built a trading empire. Solomon also beautified the capital city of Jerusalem. The crowning achievement of his building program in Jerusalem was the great temple, which he built for his god. This temple was also to be a permanent home for the Ark of the Covenant, which contained the tablets of Moses' law."

The boys' faces were a sea of puzzled frowns. This time, Marcus raised his hand. "Tablets of Moses' law! What is that? And what is an Ark of the Covenant?"

Plato nodded sagely. "I forgot to mention that part of the story." Retrieving the Moses puppet from the floor, Plato said, "This Moses received commandments from his god, describing the kind of life his people should live in order to please him. These commandments were written on stone tablets, which were housed in a sacred container called the Ark of the Covenant." Plato smiled ruefully again. "According to their own documents, they never do seem to get that right. They are always disobeying their god, especially when things were going well.

"To get back to my story, the temple that Solomon built was not large, but it gleamed like a precious gem. Bronze pillars stood at its entrance. The temple was stone on the outside, while its inner walls were made of cedar covered in gold. The main hall was richly decorated with brass and gold. Solomon even built a palace more costly and more magnificent than the temple.

"After the death of Solomon, the kingdom divided into two kingdoms, a northern kingdom called Israel and a southern kingdom called Judah. The Assyrians conquered and destroyed Israel. Then, about seven hundred years ago, the Babylonians conquered Judah. Then Nebuchadnezzar, king of Babylon, attacked Jerusalem. The city finally fell, and their temple was destroyed. The Jewish survivors were exiled to Babylon. During their exile, their prophet, Ezekiel, urged the people to keep their religion alive in a foreign land. They did keep it alive, and about fifty years later they had another change of fortune…The Persian king, Cyrus, allowed the exiles to return to Jerusalem to rebuild the temple. However, that did not last long. They disobeyed God, and he punished them by having other empires take control of their destiny."

Marcus, the only Roman citizen in the class, said boastfully, "So the Great Roman Empire is judgment upon their disobedience?"

Nicholas shoved Marcus. The two boys were the strongest boys in the class, and they were also the best of friends.

"Greece punished them first!" said Nicholas, and the two boys exchanged grins.

Ignoring the outburst, Plato said, "Herod the Great started the rebuilding of the temple in Jerusalem." Plato looked directly at Marcus. Marcus's father was a great architect in the city of Rome, and the boy demonstrated inherent ability in engineering and architecture. "Are you familiar with the story of King Herod's building projects?"

All the boys looked at Marcus. It was now his turn to cut short one of Plato's long lectures, but the boy could never deceive his beloved teacher. Besides, he was genuinely interested. Marcus said, "I don't know much about it, but I'd like to."

Smiling with delight, Plato said, "Herod the Great is transforming the city of Jerusalem as no other ruler since Solomon. He has built palaces and citadels, a theatre and amphitheatre, bridges and public monuments. These ambitious building projects, some still not complete, are increasing his capital's importance in the eyes of Rome."

Plato returned to the closet and fished about. Finally finding the object of his search, he returned to the boys. He held between his two hands a watercolor painting of the Jewish Temple.

"This was only just recently given to me," Plato said proudly. Pointing to the picture, the teacher continued, "See there, that's called the temple mount. It's a plaza for people to come and go. It's over a mile in length and width. It is surrounded by nearly a thousand columns, each thirty feet high, six feet in diameter, and each topped by a Corinthian sculpture called a capital. Look how marvelous, how beautiful." Plato pointed to one section of the painting. "You see this building with gold at the top of its columns. Now look at the platform, it's gigantic. It is so white that it glows. These buildings are quite an accomplishment. It's because of these engineering marvels that Herod got the name Herod the Great."

Marcus was a natural-born leader, and he realized that their teacher had wandered well away from the main subject of the Hebrew faith. Raising his hand again, Marcus asked, "But, Teacher, we have all heard of their magic. They sacrifice animals and birds to their god, and they burn smoky incense in their temple. They follow all kinds of obscure laws and rituals and holy days. Many people are afraid of them and their power. Why? What does it all mean?"

"Yes! Yes!" the boys chorused. They were nodding their heads in excitement. At last, someone had voiced the questions they all had about the queer Hebrew people.

Plato set aside the painting on a nearby table. He also gathered the puppets and returned them to the closet. When he was seated once again, his voice contained an unusual solemnity.

"You are right, students. This is the matter of utmost importance." Inhaling deeply, Plato continued, "At the center of their faith are several fundamentals. They believe in one perfect, all-knowing, all-powerful God, and that he created all things. He does not have a physical body, and he has existed always and will exist always. He communicates through his prophets, and the law that he gave Moses is of primary importance. They believe in divine rewards and divine retribution, based on their obedience or disobedience to that law."

Plato looked at Marcus. "This is the purpose of the sacrifices. The shedding of blood is necessary for forgiveness of their transgressions. They fast from food and drink, and they pray. Incense burning is part of their act of worship. Most of their holy days commemorate special events in their history, such as we talked about, but some holy days are to fulfill the law in worship and sacrifice to God."

Now Plato leaned forward, placing his hands on his knees, his blunt-tipped fingers spread apart. "As for their power, they would tell you that it comes from their god. And who are we to question? For they certainly have a unique power. No one can deny the strange and miraculous wonders that have surrounded them throughout their history. It is a unique phenomenon," Plato repeated. "The Jews look forward to a coming messiah, a deliverer, who will usher in a new age. Like a king, I believe. And they believe in the resurrection of the dead."

Plato did not wait for the question he knew would come. "It is tied to the coming messiah. After the messiah comes, there will be a resurrection of the dead. All those lying in dust and ashes now will rise to new life."

Plato looked around at his audience, the awestruck faces and saucer-like eyes.

• • •

Marcus felt the cooling of his skin as his sweat evaporated. The recollection of this long-ago school day from his childhood chilled him to his very bones. Now aged, Plato had nevertheless clearly seen and recognized the parallels, the possibility of Hebrew prophecy fulfilled in this investigation.

After about three hours of silence, Anthony asked, "How is it that Pilate requested you rather than his own personal guards?"

Marcus smiled. "When the Roman emperor Julius Caesar took power he initiated a new strategy to enhance Rome's ability to acquire intelligence information on the eastern tribes that were now under Rome's dominion. Caesar realized that to maintain law and order, Rome had to be able to control the tribes in the desert provinces. The army had to have reliable information regarding the possibility of rebellion.

"There is no better way of anticipating our enemies' moves than by understanding how they think. We have been trained to accomplish this mission by gathering information on these tribes and utilizing that information for anticipating their next move. This keeps us a step ahead of them. This intelligence information enhances our ability to crush any and all rebellions before they have a chance to advance past the planning stage.

Caesar had instituted a program whereby a select group of loyal centurions were trained in the culture and religious practices of the people that live in the provinces. In my case, the assignment was the Jewish quarter. It was a logical match considering my knowledge as the result of my early education with Plato.

"The assignment introduced me to my wife. The time I shared with her, though brief, brought the Hebrew history and practices to life until I lost my wife in death."

Anthony did not respond. He could see that the wound was still fresh.

Marcus felt his head pound painfully as the questions continued whirling about in his mind. *How could this be true? Had the Jewish messiah come to this world? Had Jesus been the fulfillment of all those ancient writings? Had he risen from the dead? Would Rome ever accept this theory?*

The Healing of a Servant

Situated on the north shore of the Sea of Galilee was the town of Capernaum, home of the centurion Marcus and Anthony were seeking. Capernaum was also the home town for five of Jesus' twelve disciples before they joined the itinerant prophet on his nomadic ministry, but Marcus did not think that information pertained to his case today. The centurion, however, may have some light to shed, at least, according to Plato.

The soldiers inquired as to the whereabouts of the centurion, named Cornelius, and they were directed to a stone villa with a lovely view of the shore. At the house's front entrance they were greeted by a Jewish servant.

"May I help you?"

"We are looking for the Centurion Cornelius. We were advised this is his residence," answered Anthony.

"Yes, it is," responded the servant. "Come in. I will summon him. He is in his vineyard with his wife and children."

While they waited in the foyer, the men admired the construction of the large home. A dozen marble pillars stood sentry along the front. The exterior walls were made of basalt, and the floors were lined with a thin layer of decorated plaster. A series of adjoining rooms formed the perimeter of the rectangular-shaped house, with two grand courtyards in the center. The courtyards were separated by a splendid garden. A stone walkway in the garden led to a brick oven, indicating the family's enjoyment of cooking and eating outdoors, for a chimney on the eastern side of the house revealed the interior cooking room.

The walls displayed colorful mosaics, and the two soldiers were appraising the artwork when Cornelius entered. The man was obviously puzzled by their appearance, but the Roman uniform put him at ease. Cornelius extended his hand and introduced himself.

"I am Cornelius. What can I do to assist you?"

After introducing themselves, Marcus spoke.

"We have been assigned by Governor Pilate to investigate the disappearance of the corpse of Jesus from a tomb that was sealed and secured by Roman authority.."

"We were informed that you may have pertinent information concerning this Jesus," added Anthony.

Appearing troubled, Cornelius responded, "I had some interaction with him in the past. Frankly, I'm shocked by his death." Wagging his heavy head in disbelief, Cornelius continued, "Please sit. Would you like a drink?"

Marcus and Anthony followed Cornelius to a nearby room where the three men sat down in elaborately designed, thickly cushioned chairs. From a sideboard, Cornelius poured wine into three goblets. Anthony remarked on the beauty of Cornelius's home, but the centurion did not respond. He was preoccupied with thoughts of the man he had met, and who was now dead.

"I don't know where to begin," Cornelius said. "Why are you here questioning me? Why wouldn't the guards that were stationed at the tomb be able to point you in the direction of the thieves? Unless, they have been wounded? Are the guards still alive?"

Answering himself, Cornelius stated, "How in the world could they be alive if they were confronted by rebel thieves? Either the thieves would have been killed or the soldiers."

"With all due respect," said Marcus, "this is a complicated investigation, and we don't have the time to explain all the intricacies. We are simply interested in your contact with Jesus."

"With all due respect," retorted Cornelius, "you have traveled to my home to question me about a missing corpse. I have treated you with dignity and respect. I expect you to do the same. If you want me to cooperate with your investigation, I want to know what this is all about. If you expect me to believe that this is just about a missing corpse, you may want to reconsider." Lowering his massive head and glaring at Anthony from underneath his bushy brows, the stout man demanded, "Bore me with the details."

Anthony glanced at Marcus, who nodded in the affirmative. Anthony continued, "At the beginning of this investigation it appeared to be routine. Certainly the body had been stolen, and the thieves would be his followers. However, the deeper we've gotten into this the more complicated it has become. We have interviewed most of the witnesses to the crucifixion and the burial. So far we have verified that Jesus was dead and was placed in a tomb.

"The tomb was secured and protected by Roman and temple guards. His followers are quite convinced that he has risen from the dead; they've even reported seeing him."

Anthony waited for Cornelius to comment, but when he did not he continued.

"They even spent time attempting to convince us through their holy book that this was predicted. Frankly, they make a good case. Although we are not convinced by their argument, we have decided to look at this from a different perspective. Rather than attempting to find the body we are now attempting to determine who this Jesus was. We were advised that you had contact with him and witnessed an astonishing event. We thought it would be worth traveling up here to find out exactly what occurred. We thought that your testimony would be important and valid. As a soldier of Rome, you have no reason to lie or exaggerate your contact with him."

Marcus asked, "So then, is that enough information to get your cooperation?"

Sitting back in his chair with a look of peaceful contentment, Cornelius smiled and said, "Yes. That is enough information to get my cooperation. It would be my pleasure, more than you might know, to explain what I witnessed concerning this Jesus. I have lived in this area for so many years I have almost forgotten what Rome looks like. As you can see, I have been blessed with wealth. I have many Jewish servants. Because of them I have some knowledge of their God and their beliefs.

"During the past three years, the servants have been telling me about this Jesus and all the signs and wonders he performed. On several occasions I myself watched from a distance. I even went so far as to have my servants interpret their holy book.

"A few months ago one of my servants, whom I love like a son, became very sick. It was apparent to my household that he was going to die. I had heard that Jesus had just arrived in Capernaum. I summoned my servants, who told their elders and requested help from Jesus. I was waiting for word from them when I became very anxious. I decided to meet them on their return. As I approached I saw them proceeding toward me. Apparently he was coming to my home. As he walked up to me he said he would come to my home and heal my servant."

Cornelius raised his stocky bulk from the chair and stood with a look of wonder in his eyes. "It is hard for me to describe what I felt. His words had power. He spoke with authority.

> I said to him, "Lord, do not trouble yourself further, for I am not worthy for you to come under my roof,…but just say the word, and my servant will be healed. For indeed, I am a man under authority, with soldiers under me; and I say to this one, 'Go!' and he goes, and to another, 'Come!' and he comes, and to my slave, 'Do this!' and he does it." When Jesus heard this, He marveled at me. He turned to the crowd and said, "I say to you, not even in Israel have I found such great faith. Go your way; let it be done to you as you have believed."
> Luke 7: 6-9 (NASV)

"When I returned home my servant was healed. Completely recovered! I asked those who were present with my servant exactly when he recovered. When they told me, I was not surprised. I knew! He did it by the authority and power that was in him!"

Cornelius' voice took on a ring of fiery faith. "I was convinced then as I am now that Jesus was more than a man. When you first reported to me that his crucified body was missing, I felt in my soul tremendous pain; but I knew that there had to be more to it. When you decided to explain more fully what occurred, you convinced me that he is still alive!"

Cornelius moved behind his chair and leaned upon the back for support.

"I could testify to so much about his life. Most of his ministry was in this area. Miracles, signs, and wonders, things that he did that a mere man could never accomplish. Gentlemen, I would have to agree with his disciples. It does not astonish me that this Jesus may have risen from the dead.

"The Hebrew God is a totally different being from our Roman gods and the Greek gods. Their God desires a relationship with mankind. Everywhere you turn in the Hebrew book you see a rebellious people in a relationship with a compassionate God who never seems to give up on them.

"Even His commandments that were given to their prophet Moses demonstrate his goodwill toward His people. When I examined their ten commandments it is clear to me that they are beyond human invention." Cornelius raised his index finger to the ceiling and boomed in a thunderous voice, "In fact, that brings back a memory of an event I witnessed between Jesus and a lawyer. In this particular event, which I witnessed, this Jewish lawyer asked Jesus what he should do to inherit eternal life. Jesus responded to the question with a question. 'What is written in the law?' The lawyer appeared well versed in the law and quoted his Hebrew book. 'You shall love the Lord your God with all your heart, soul, mind, and strength, and your neighbor as yourself.' Jesus said, 'You have answered correctly: do this and you will live.' But this lawyer wanted to justify himself.

He said to Jesus, 'Who is my neighbor?' Jesus told a story about a man who fell among robbers. They stripped him and beat him and left him half dead. By chance a certain priest was going on that road, and when he saw him, he passed on the other side. And then a Levite noticed the beaten man, and he too passed on the other side. Then a Samaritan, who is considered by the Jews a half-breed with no religious knowledge, came upon the beaten man and felt compassion. He bandaged up his wounds, poured oil and wine on them, put the man on his own beast and brought him to an inn, and took care of him. The next day he gave the innkeeper money and told him to take care of the man and said, 'Whatever more it costs when I return, I will repay you.' Then Jesus looked directly at the lawyer and asked, 'Which of the three do you think proved to

be a neighbor to the man that fell into the robbers' hands?'
Luke 10:29-36 (NASV)

"The lawyer was asking Jesus, '*Who is my neighbor?*' but Jesus turned the question around; rather than the abstract question of who is my neighbor, he wanted the lawyer to understand that there is a more important question: *To whom can I be a neighbor?*

"Do you see the depth of that conversation? It wasn't a question of who's my neighbor. The real issue is who I can be a neighbor to? This is beyond mere human insight. This Jesus saw into the depths of men's hearts. He wanted them to understand the deeper meanings of life. Life is much more than what is seen by the eyes."

Cornelius breathed laboriously and eyed the men in their chairs. "I would be remiss if I didn't tell you what I believe is true concerning him. I think one must ask himself an important question. Is this life nothing more than a mere accident, or is there a greater power at work, an invisible power that has an exact plan?"

Cornelius circled the chair and lowered himself back onto the cushion. "One last thing I would ask you to consider for your own personal edification. If God was to become a man, what kind of man would he be?"

Marcus and Anthony stood speechless.

Cornelius continued, "To my way of thinking, his character would have to be flawless. He would have to have entered history in a unique way. He would have to perform supernatural acts that a mere man could not. His words would be deep yet simple, capable of piercing the very heart of a man. And beyond that he would have to be able to destroy man's most feared enemy—*death*. I have met great men in my career. Honorable, loyal, faithful, truthful, compassionate, strong. Jesus had all of these character traits. But even more important than these, it seems that if God became man, whatever he would *speak to, it would obey*. In other words, he would have the power and authority to accomplish whatever he wished…healing the sick, changing water into wine, or raising the dead back to life. If God became man, none of those accomplishments would be more difficult than the other. How could they be? The use of power would not diminish his energy, would it?

Then the other question one might ask is why would he become a man? The idea of a king becoming a servant is fascinating. That would be an immeasurable act of love. According to the Jewish history, God kept sending them prophets, and they were mistreated or killed. Or those messengers would fall into the sin of misrepresenting the person of God and his message. Maybe he decided to come himself so there would be no mistake about who he is and what he said."

Cornelius's voice had softened considerably, and now he smiled.

"I apologize for getting philosophical. His memory raises these thoughts in me."

Marcus and Anthony both stood up so quickly that Cornelius was startled. Marcus said, "You have given us much insight. We appreciate your hospitality and openness. We must take our leave, for there is much to do in order to complete this investigation."

"Are you all right?" asked Cornelius. "It was not my intention to overwhelm you."

"I miss the days of simple questions," joked Anthony.

"Listen," said Cornelius. "When you step out you will be swallowed in the life that is your world. I challenge you both to find time—time alone, to consider the possibility that you are investigating the most important event in human history."

Cornelius called for his servant. "Simon will show you to the door."

Marcus and Anthony returned to their horses and headed back in the direction of Jerusalem. They were going to interrogate the temple guards.

When they arrived at the temple, their detective instincts told the men that they were being watched, and soon they became aware of the guards and servants of the priests huddled together with their eyes fixed on the approaching soldiers. Suddenly one of the servants broke free of the group and began a fast walk toward the temple mount, keeping his eyes on the soldiers.

With a grin Anthony turned to Marcus. "I got him."

He dismounted and made his way toward the retreating servant. As Anthony advanced the servant began to run. Anthony continued his pursuit and caught up with the servant at the entrance to the temple.

Anthony threw him on the steps that led to the entrance of the temple and began slapping him across the face. Within seconds, Marcus caught up to them.

"It seems you're in a bit of a hurry," he said. Grabbing the servant by his throat, Marcus asked, "What is your name, and why did you run?"

Visibly shaking, the young man replied, "I am Malchus, a servant of the high priests, and I am late—"

Anthony slapped him on the head and demanded, "Do you know the guards that were assigned to the tomb of Jesus? If you lie I will cut your tongue out."

"I know the guard; his name is Saul. He was assigned to the tomb along with the Roman guards." Looking in all directions as he spoke, Malchus continued, "Please let me go; I will get in trouble for talking with you. We have been warned by the priests of your investigation. They have made it clear to all of us that we would pay a hefty price if we cooperated with this investigation. We are told to direct any questions from the Roman authority to them. You must understand that we would be ostracized for giving our opinion concerning this Jesus. We Jews have only one another. None of us would survive alone. Please have mercy on me."

"We will torture you in ways that are unimaginable if we don't get what we want." Raising his voice after each word Anthony continued, "You will tell us the whole truth regarding your knowledge of Jesus. Am I making myself clear?"

Malchus pleaded, "If I tell you what I witnessed, will you promise me anonymity? I will even tell you where to find Saul. But I must be assured of my safety."

"Your testimony will be part of our investigation. However, we will not reveal your identity. There is no reason for us to identify you to your superiors. That's the best we can do," said Anthony.

Malchus glanced about. "I guess that will have to do."

The scuffle had drawn some attention, but confrontations between the Romans and the Jews were a common occurrence, so most people had quickly looked away and continued on their business.

To deflect any further attention, Malchus, smoothing his wet palms on the front of his tunic, murmured through tight lips, "Follow me through this door. It will take us outside."

• • •

Outside the temple wall, Malchus ducked into a shaded alcove. He spun around to face the soldiers. Satisfied that they did not intend to harm him, the slender man rested his back against the cool wall. He cupped one elbow with the opposite hand and rested his chin in the uplifted hand. Malchus was resigned to the situation. He would have to divulge his remarkable story to these soldiers even though he had been expressly forbidden to do so by the high priests, Annas and Caiaphas. In a way, Malchus was relieved. The tale had been dancing on the end of his tongue for days. At last, it could be released.

Perhaps he should not have run. That had drawn their attention. But, perhaps, he had wanted to draw their attention, so that he could tell his story.

Malchus began, "My first actual contact with Jesus was the night before his crucifixion. There was a conspiracy between the chief priests and one of Jesus' disciples. His name was Judas. He was going to identify Jesus to the chief priests while Jesus was meeting with his followers at the Mount of Olives. Many soldiers from the temple guards were assigned to arrest him. It was very dark that night; it seemed blacker than most nights. I carried a torch, but others had swords and clubs."

Malchus gasped, and his voice took on a breathy texture. "The next thing I remember I was on my knees with blood flowing down the side of my face. One of his followers had cut off my ear! Jesus took command of the situation and ordered his followers not to resist."

The young man with his womanish gestures began to cry. Wringing his hands in distress, Malchus said, "There was no reason for him to help me. I was there to assist in the arrest, yet he showed compassion on me. He helped me up, reached down and picked up my ear and placed it back where it belonged."

The investigators' faces remained hard and unrevealing.

Malchus said, "I know you don't believe me, but other people saw it. But when we returned, the priests insisted that it was a magic trick, a trick of the devil. We were threatened not to make mention of it again."

Malchus's face and voice were somber. "There is much talk in the community regarding the possibility of Jesus having risen from the dead. It's causing much excitement and anxiety to our priests. So Saul's been ordered to keep out of sight. He stays underground here at the temple."

"Does he ever leave?" asked Marcus.

"Yes, he does. The priests don't know it, but I myself have witnessed Saul leaving the temple during the early morning hours to visit his mistress who lives a stone's throw from here. Please, you promised that you would keep my identity secret. You gave me your word."

"We have no intention of revealing your identity to anyone," Anthony said. "We appreciate your cooperation; we will take it from here. However, we do need an accurate description of him. We can't do much with your information without the ability to identify Saul."

"That will be easy. He is a most conspicuous individual. Once you've seen him it's hard to forget him. He's around thirty years old, but he looks like he's fifty.

He lingers long over wine, which has produced an extra large stomach and a wobble in his walk. He is very short, maybe five feet tall, with a slightly hunched back. He has a long straggly beard. It's usually between two and three in the morning that he makes his way to her home."

They released the servant and began making plans for an all-night surveillance. The men decided to set up on opposite sides of the street, in locations that gave them the capability to trap Saul once he walked inside their perimeter.

• • •

Back on their horses, they headed to an inn for a meal. They could leave their horses secured at the inn's stable until they returned. They stayed at the inn until night fell; then they proceeded to their positions.

Hidden in the landscape, Marcus was safe and secure from onlookers. He had stationed himself where he could observe anyone exiting or entering the temple. All directions were completely covered.

On the other side of the street, Anthony had also set up his position. He had rolled in the dirt and poured wine on his clothes so that he would appear to be drunk. Anthony was excited about the possible outcome of the surveillance. He was hoping that Saul would attempt to flee, and he would have the opportunity of running him down.

Both men stared at the moonlight reflecting off the temple wall and thought about the progress of the investigation. Anthony was coming to believe that this Jesus could very well be more than a mere human. He did not think that all the information they had gathered would be nullified by what Saul and the other guards witnessed. He had become convinced after John made his argument concerning the prophecies. When Plato laid out his theories it confirmed his belief.

Anthony had not yet mentioned anything to Marcus, fearing his disappointment, but he promised himself that when the time was right he would make his perspective known. He really wanted Marcus to see what he had come to believe, but he knew that he must not force the issue.

Just as Malchus had said, during the early hours of the morning Anthony noticed movement from the entranceway of the temple. Out of the shadows the two men observed a figure that matched the description Malchus had given them.

As the shadowy figure passed through the perimeter, Anthony and Marcus moved toward him. Saul became aware of their presence and began to shuffle quickly away.

Anthony lunged and grabbed Saul from behind, wrapping his arms tightly around his mouth and throat.

Anthony then lifted Saul off his feet and threw him to the ground. It sounded like thunder. When he hit the ground his head shot back and slammed into a concrete step. Immediately he fell unconscious, and the men noticed blood pooling around his head.

"Now what?" growled Marcus, barely containing his fury. "We finally apprehend someone who was actually at the tomb, and you probably killed him."

"I resent that, Marcus. Look here." Reaching toward Saul's waist, Anthony retrieved a dagger. "That's what he was going for. So now what do you have to say? I saved you from getting filleted like a fish."

Marcus never took his eyes from Saul, who was regaining consciousness.

"Get him up, Anthony, and move him into this alleyway."

Throwing Saul's arms around their shoulders, they stumbled into the alleyway like three drunks, in case anyone was watching. In the alley they let Saul slide to the ground with his back against the wall. Turning to Anthony, Marcus said, "You saved me from him? Please!"

Saul moaned and attempted to focus his eyes on the two men standing before him. Anthony placed his foot on his neck and warned him not to try escaping. Then removing his foot, Anthony asked, "You are Saul, the temple guard?"

Frantically Saul babbled, "No, not at all. Why does that matter? Does that matter? Are you not mere robbers looking to steal my hard-earned money? What does it matter who I am? How is it that you know who I am? Who are you? What do you want of me?" Observing their Roman garments, and the dirt and smell of Anthony, Saul continued, "Who are you? What business do you have with me?"

"This is Anthony, and I am Marcus. We have spent many days attempting to find you and a couple of other guards. We have some questions regarding your assignment last week to the tomb of Jesus."

Saul flew up from the ground in an amazing burst of sudden strength and tried to push his way past the soldiers. He was screaming, "*I know nothing about that night! Help! Someone! Help! I'm being attacked!*"

Marcus punched Saul in the head, knocking him to the ground. Sitting on the little man's chest and squeezing his throat, Marcus snarled, "I will rip your windpipe right out of your throat if you don't calm down."

Saul shook his head. Marcus eased up on his throat, and Saul began to catch his breath.

Slowly, Marcus released him and allowed Saul to rest his back against the wall once more. When he could speak, Saul said, "I am a temple guard, and you have no right or jurisdiction over me. I demand to be brought to the temple where I can make my defense. I will not be questioned on the street like a common criminal. I am also a Roman citizen. That means I have rights."

"Listen carefully, you little maggot," Anthony said as he grabbed Saul by the shoulders and shoved him hard. "We have the seal of Pilate, which means we have the power and authority of Rome to investigate and get to the bottom of this case. Now I tell you the truth, I will at this very moment stick my sword through your chin and out the back of your head if you don't cooperate. Now, I will explain this to you slowly and methodically. You will shut your big pig mouth and only answer the questions that you're asked. If you even make the slightest mistake, I will without hesitation pierce you until you squeal like the pig that you are. Do we understand each other?" When Saul nodded, Anthony said, "I thought so. Why don't you tell us all about your adventure the night that Jesus was placed in the rich man's tomb? You remember that, don't you?"

Trembling and sweating profusely, Saul cried, "That night is a little foggy! I was drinking, and I'm not sure what happened!"

Anthony responded with several blows to the little man's face.

"How did you like that?" Punching him again several more times, Anthony said, "How did you like that? I will kill you now with my bare hands. I can beat you all night until I get the truth or until you die." Punching him again and again, Anthony said to Marcus, "Would you like to take a turn? It's rather exhilarating."

"You win!" screamed Saul. "I am afraid! I fear for my life! You have no idea what will happen to me if I cooperate with you. I will be tortured, killed! My family will be ostracized from the community. Either way I am a dead man." Saul began weeping, "I have no way out. I have no way out."

Anthony whispered into the ear of the guard, "Saul, are you not a believer in the one God? Wouldn't your God want you to tell the truth? Do you not sacrifice animals to your God for forgiveness of your sins? Can this God forgive you if you willfully lie or deny the truth? Isn't your God more important than the temple priests? I have heard that your God is a God of truth, is that so?"

"Yes, yes, he is a God of truth."

"Well then, does he not expect his servants to be truthful?"

Saul was quiet for several moments. Then he answered, "Yes, he does expect his children to be truthful, yes…I'm only stating what I saw. How can that displease God? I can't tell you anything about the night Jesus was laid in the tomb. I was dispatched to the tomb the next day, after the Sabbath. The priests wanted to make sure that the tomb was secure and protected. When I arrived at the scene there were several soldiers in the vicinity. We temple guards don't have the best relationship with the Romans, as I'm sure you know. When we arrived the entrance rock was in its original place and the Roman guards were about to seal the tomb. There were dozens of guards for the event. They stretched a cord across the stone and sealed each end with sealing clay, and then using your official stamp of the procurator they pressed it into the waxy substance. When all was said and done it was evident that Rome's power and authority were behind the protection of this tomb. It is quite a ceremony you Romans put on. There was nothing that occurred that was out of the ordinary, at least in the beginning of the night. I guess we must have fallen asleep because when we awakened the body was missing. And so we thought that the disciples probably stole it. Yes, we were sure that the disciples stole him."

Marcus looked at Anthony in disbelief.

"We just got done beating his pig face into the ground, and now he is going to start his nonsense all over again."

"No, not at all," protested Saul. "We fell asleep, and when we awoke the body was missing. Ask your own guards. They will tell you the same story. His disciples sneaked up on us. They are very cunning rebels. Yes, they are known for such bold and aggressive acts."

As Anthony and Marcus reached down to grab Saul, they became aware of movement from all directions. Dozens of men wielding clubs and swords approached Marcus and Anthony. The soldiers drew their swords and prepared to engage the crowd. From the midst of the crowd came a voice.

"*Stop*! There is no need for violence."

As the crowd slowly parted for the owner of the voice, a man of majestic bearing, in long black robes, stood speaking to the two men.

"I am High Priest Caiaphas, and we are not here to cause you harm. We only wish to have our guard Saul returned to our custody. He is under our authority, and if he has broken any of the laws we will punish him. If he has broken Roman law, he has a right to trial because he is a Roman citizen."

Handing Caiaphas the letter with the Roman seal, Marcus explained, "Saul is in our custody. As you can see, the letter makes it clear that we have the authority and power to arrest and take into custody anyone, including this little worm. I suggest you make way. This is going to get very ugly very quickly."

"Pilate does not have authority over my guards. There is a policy and procedure that has been in place since Rome took control of this region. Even Pilate cannot supercede it. We demand you release him and go your way."

While Caiaphas held the attention of the crowd, Anthony had stealthily closed in on him from behind. The soldier now grabbed the high priest in a choke hold and put his sword to the side of his neck. At the same time, Marcus grabbed Saul and placed his sword to the throat of the guard. Smiling, Marcus said, "Well now, things seem to be getting very interesting."

The crowd fell back, bringing down their clubs and swords.

Anthony's grin grew wider, and he said, "This is very exciting, Marcus! Marcus, may I begin to filet my man now? I may eat his liver after I cut out his heart."

Underneath the many layers of black robes, Caiaphas felt the humiliating rush of warm urine coursing down his leg. It made a thunderous sound against the dry, packed earth, and the man's mortification was complete. He closed his eyes and pleaded, "Please don't harm me." To the crowd he shouted, "Leave! Leave at once! No one is to attempt to stop these soldiers!"

Tightening his grip on Caiaphas, Anthony said, "You're coming with us, Caiaphas, and so is Saul."

"We will release you when we are at a safe distance," said Marcus. "However, Saul will be accompanying us to the garrison where we will continue our investigation."

Keeping their prisoners securely in their grasp, Anthony and Marcus hustled them to the waiting horses at the nearby inn. After galloping several miles Anthony threw Caiaphas off his horse.

From his prone position on the ground, he shouted after them, "Herod will hear about this! We will see who has the last laugh."

Marcus brought his horse to an abrupt stop. Caiaphas, petrified, rose to his feet and began running. Marcus drew his sword, but Anthony yelled, "Let him go. I'm hungry and exhausted."

Marcus shrugged and replaced his sword. "When we get to the garrison we will turn him over to the prison guards and get some rest." Realizing how filthy and blood-spattered they were, Marcus added, "Maybe we should bathe first."

Pilate and Herod

It was just past dawn, and already the hot rays of the orange sun baked the landscape as Pilate sat eating his breakfast. Reaching for his goblet of fresh berry juice, he watched the shimmering waves of heat rise from the desert floor. A sudden stirring of the torrid air, and Pilate knew his breakfast would go unfinished. Demetrios would not dare to disturb his morning meal for a minor matter.

Demetrios fell on one knee and bowed his head. "So sorry to disturb you, Your Majesty, but I was informed by Herod's servant that he wishes to see you this afternoon. He has an urgent matter to discuss with you."

Pilate forked a mound of eggs into his mouth and chewed furiously. After a few moments, he barked, "Is that all?"

"The servant would not give me any more details," replied Demetrios. As he rose to his feet, he ventured, "I wonder, my lord, if it has to do with your investigation."

"I'm sure it does," Pilate muttered. "The only reason he would request an audience with me is to attempt to humiliate me. He is a snake. He must have acquired some information regarding Marcus's investigation."

Pilate threw down his cutlery. The eggs had turned to rubber in his mouth, and he found he no longer had an appetite.

"I have not heard from Marcus for several days. Demetrios, I need you to locate him and have him meet me here at the palace. We need to know what has been uncovered by his investigation before Herod arrives. I don't want to be caught off guard by some new revelation regarding the missing body. Go directly to the garrison and ascertain if anyone knows his location. *Go! Hurry! Report back immediately!*" And Pilate waved the servant off with a shooing motion of his hand.

While he waited, Pilate paced about the palace. The deadliest of enemies before the crucifixion debacle, he and Herod had recently become rather cordial, allies before the common enemy of the Jewish piety. Still, Pilate did not trust the arrogant, pompous, self-important, self-indulgent tetrarch of Galilee. He would never show Herod his back.

"Where is that Marcus?" Pilate ruminated. *He better have some pertinent information. He was supposed to keep me informed. It has been several days. He will pay a heavy price if I am humiliated by Herod.*

Pilate wiped sweat from his brow and cursed the heat. He never would get used to this climate.

At the garrison, Demetrios was directed to a sleeping area located below ground. In the cavernous room he observed hundreds of cots and cast-off soldiers' uniforms carpeting the floor. Dozens of soldiers slumbered in between shifts and assignments. Demetrios walked silently among the cots, looking for Marcus or Anthony. It did not take long for him to recognize the blue-black hair of Marcus and the blonde curls of his younger partner. Both men were snoring raucously, but when Demetrios stopped alongside Marcus's cot, the soldier sat up immediately, as though an inner alarm had been tripped. He frowned at the servant.

"Demetrios?"

"Yes, my lord, it is I. The governor directed me to find you and Anthony. He has ordered you both to his palace immediately. He has been informed that Herod has requested an audience with him this afternoon. He is concerned that Herod has uncovered new information regarding this investigation. He wants to meet with you before Herod arrives. We must make haste. The governor is waiting."

Marcus looked over at the cot on which Anthony still slept. Fortunately, they had washed themselves and cleaned up their uniforms before hitting the cots.

"Anthony!" hissed Marcus. Anthony's snoring ceased abruptly, and he lazily opened one eye. "Get dressed. We must go to the palace immediately. Herod has requested a meeting with Pilate, and Pilate wants an update from us."

Anthony rolled onto his side and propped himself on one elbow.

"That's insane. We finally have gotten custody of this temple guard. Why don't we interview him first? We may finally get some real answers."

Demetrios bristled. Although he was a servant, he resented the overrated soldiers. And his loyalty to Pilate was total. "The governor is waiting," he repeated, through tightly clenched teeth.

Anthony laughed. "Go back to the palace, Demetrios. Tell the governor we will be along directly. There's a good boy now."

Demetrios spun on his heels and stalked out, his rage evident in each pounding step. Anthony laughed harder, and Marcus shook his head.

"That wasn't wise, Anthony. Pilate seems to favor him."

Anthony shrugged in a careless manner. The servant did not concern him. Neither did Pilate, for that matter.

The two men stood and rapidly dressed. Marcus ordered Anthony to locate Julius and inquire about the Roman guards. "They should be back from Joppa by now," he said.

• • •

On the way to the palace, Marcus spoke.

"Anthony, you must not offer any information regarding our investigation. I mean it. You will not open up your mouth concerning anything that we have uncovered. I want you to show no emotion. I realize that you are perplexed regarding the facts that we have uncovered; nonetheless, you must not give way to any conclusions regarding the missing body.

"We still have not interviewed the most important witnesses of them all—our own Roman guards. Their statement may shed new light into this investigation. Therefore, for our sakes and for the sake of your family, do nothing but agree with everything that I say."

The younger man stared at Marcus. Finally, he said, "I understand your concern, but don't you think that Pilate has a right to know the direction of this investigation? There is a tremendous amount of evidence that an unusual event has taken place. Maybe Pilate will embrace the possibility that this Jesus was more than just a man."

"*Anthony! Shut your mouth!* This is exactly what I mean. You have this naive notion that people are interested in the truth. That is false. People are interested in their own personal glory. Their own power. Their own reputation. Haven't you learned anything from me? Man has raised himself up in his own mind. Study history. It's the same story over and over. Empires come and go. Men of power set themselves up as gods. Then they fall, and others set themselves up as gods. And if they find that this does not fulfill their ambitions, they make up gods to fit their plans. Do you not see that the so-called gods are merely a mirror of man? Have we not previously discussed this? The gods are made in the image of man. They are invented so that one man can manipulate another. Now then, you will shut your mouth and keep your opinion to yourself. In fact, you will shut up now. Do not speak another word to me. That's an order. And do not open your mouth to Pilate."

For the remainder of the short trip to the palace, not a word was spoken between the men. Anthony had never felt such anger. He was very close to insubordination. He wanted to retaliate for the disrespect Marcus had shown him. Anthony feared no man, and by the time they reached the palace, he had convinced himself that the only way to regain his honor was to fight Marcus, even to the death.

Marcus knew that he had gone too far in his rebuke. He loved Anthony and saw much of himself in the younger man, but he knew that Anthony needed to learn of whom he should beware. Anthony's lack of restraint with the wrong person, such as Pilate, could destroy them and put Anthony's family at risk. The way Anthony had baited Pilate's servant was an example of the impulsive behavior that could land him in severe trouble.

Besides, Marcus had more experience dealing with Pilate. He knew that Pilate would look at Anthony's theory concerning the possibility of this Jesus being more than a mere man as nothing but a threat to himself and his authority. Marcus knew that Pilate destroyed threats.

Marcus intended to tread lightly when advising Pilate of their investigation. He fully understood the ramifications of a man rising from the dead, who claimed he was God. If this were true it would change everything, all of history. Rome would be obligated to submit to this new authority. Marcus grew overwhelmed and agitated with such thoughts and shook them out of his mind. He then turned to Anthony; but Anthony faced forward, his shoulders squared, his spine rigid.

Demetrios met them at the palace gates.

"Come this way. Pilate is awaiting your arrival."

Marcus, attempting friendliness, asked, "How does he appear?"

"Very anxious. He is concerned about Herod's intentions. Here we are." Turning to the governor, who sat in a chair sipping wine, Demetrios asked, "Is there anything else, Your Highness?"

"No, Demetrios, that will be all for now."

When the servant had exited, Pilate said sarcastically, "My apologies for disturbing you. You must be very busy that you could not find the time to inform me of my investigation. Isn't that correct, Marcus?"

"Your Highness, I apologize for the delay, but the investigation was much more complicated than we first surmised. Between the traveling and the dozens of interviews, it has taken more time than we anticipated. Just last night we got in a physical confrontation with Caiaphas and his temple guards."

Pilate frowned so deeply his face became a mass of angry folds from which his flinty black eyes regarded the soldiers.

"What do you mean, Marcus? Caiaphas hampered your investigation?"

"Absolutely! Every time we have attempted to locate someone whom we believed was significant in this investigation, we have been hampered by him or his followers. If it weren't for our alertness, they would have killed us last night."

Pilate let his gaze fall on Anthony while he contemplated Marcus's words. Then he said, "Why would he do such a thing? He should be as interested in finding the missing body as I am. Unless, he is in agreement with Herod to destroy me? Yes, that makes sense. They have conspired to humiliate me."

Marcus said, "Your Highness, we are very close to a conclusion to this investigation. At this moment we have in custody at the garrison a temple guard who was at the scene of the crime when the body was stolen. I promise you that this guard will give us the facts. We were just about to interview him when Demetrios informed us you wanted to see us. Also, you should be aware that one of Herod's men hampered our investigation early on. He is the captain at the garrison. I had to fight him in order to gain access to the garrison. We still have not been able to interview the two Roman guards that were stationed at the tomb that weekend. We were told they were dispatched with others to Joppa to quell a disturbance. The captain could have assisted us by ordering their quick return; instead he threatened to report us to Herod. So as you can see we have been blocked by both Herod and Caiaphas from beginning to end. And it is because of them that we did not report back as we should have. We were doing everything in our power to acquire pertinent information for you before we reported to you. We were embarrassed at our lack of success, and I apologize."

Pilate began pacing the floor and ranting to himself.

"Now I understand...I realize I was abrupt... It appeared that you were not being diligent with this investigation. Obviously, I was wrong. I now see that Herod is the impediment. It is clear that there is a conspiracy to ruin my name and usurp my authority. That is probably why he has requested an audience with me today." Pilate's lower lip protruded as he sat thinking for a few moments. Then he said, "Marcus I want you to return to the garrison to complete your investigation. You will be accompanied by a dozen of my guards. They will be under your command. If this captain or anyone else does anything to impede your investigation I want them arrested and brought to me. In the meantime I will dispatch other soldiers to ascertain when the other two guards will return. If they are still stationed in Joppa I will have them relieved of their duty and report to you at the garrison. Make haste; I want this investigation completed."

Marcus and Anthony left Pilate's presence. As they mounted the horses Marcus's eyes kept turning toward

Anthony, but the younger man kept his distance and pointedly ignored him. Clumsy with emotion, Marcus was at a loss as to how to make amends with his partner, who had grown to be his friend. He tried clearing his throat several times, but the noisy cacophony brought no response from Anthony.

"I'm sorry!" Marcus finally shouted.

Anthony turned his face toward Marcus, but his eyes remained veiled.

In a softer voice, Marcus continued, "Anthony, I'm sorry for speaking to you in that manner. I know that you are an honorable man. I did not mean to disrespect you or your name."

Anthony nodded and looked away, but Marcus wasn't finished. He had more to say.

"Anthony, you are a noble man. A man who is interested in the truth. Your courage and faithfulness have never come into question. But sometimes, in this life, being honest and pure can get you killed. You must believe me when I tell you that these politicians are ruthless, self-centered, and willing to do anything to protect their power and authority. So you must keep in mind that truth is irrelevant to them if it does not promote their own goals and ambitions."

After several moments of silence Anthony said, "I accept your apology." Anthony's voice held an edge of hardness. "But I must tell you that I will not be disrespected like that again."

Marcus acknowledged Anthony's statement with a curt bow of his head.

"By the way…" Anthony's voice now held the familiar ring of humor, and Marcus was relieved to know that the incident had passed. "How did you come up with that conspiracy theory? Pilate swallowed it whole."

"Ah," Marcus waved his hand dismissively, "all these politicians think the same. They are convinced that someone is plotting against them." With a burst of laughter, Marcus said, "You just have to know what the animal feeds on."

At that moment, Marcus and Anthony saw a group of soldiers standing by the roadside a short distance away. One lifted his hand, and Marcus recognized that these were the soldiers Pilate had ordered to accompany them to the garrison. He lifted his hand in response.

"It will be interesting to see how the captain at the garrison reacts to this," said Anthony with a laugh.

• • •

Pilate felt prepared for Herod's arrival now that he had met with Marcus and Anthony. He had commanded his servants to set up a room for a feast with plenty of food and wine and entertainment. Herod would be accompanied by his perverted entourage, but Pilate was determined to affect an air of tranquil conviviality.

He entered the room, now empty, and seated himself to await his guests. He reached for a decanter of wine and tilted it back. He was still holding the decanter when Demetrios approached him.

"Your Highness, Herod has arrived with several others. Should I send them in?"

"Yes, Demetrios. Also, have my guards station themselves around the perimeter of the palace. And then return to me. I want you to witness this charade."

When Herod and his fawning band of revelers swept into the room, Pilate could hardly hide his revulsion and had to swallow another mouthful of wine to settle his nauseated stomach. As a military man, a man's man, he was disgusted by Herod and his orgiastic followers.

Reputed to be a womanizer, Herod would eventually be brought to ruin by his desire for and marriage to his brother's wife, who was also his niece, Herodias. It was reported that lust for Herodias's daughter, Salome, had resulted in the beheading of the righteous man John the Baptist, for Salome had danced for Herod's birthday and so pleased him that he offered to give her whatever she wished. She requested the head of the Baptist at the urging of her mother. Yet Herod's appearance and mannerisms were overtly effeminate.

Today, the tetrarch was dressed flamboyantly in women's garments. He wore a stole made of silk, a very expensive material imported from China that was used exclusively by women. The silk was dyed a deep purple, the color of gods and emperors. The stole was clasped along the sides by gold brooches so highly polished they sparkled.

Herod wore a king's crown of gold on his head, but beneath the crown was a thick blonde wig. Around his neck flashed an ornate, jeweled necklace that matched his earrings, many bracelets, and rings. On his face, he wore cosmetics, chalk powder, charcoal, and saffron. His feet were shod with indoor slippers made of silk and decorated with pearls. The slippers indicated that he had arrived on a litter, carried by his slaves.

"My dear Pilate, how good it is to see you. It's been too long. I see you've done a fine job of decorating. You must send your decorator to me. I have so many unfinished rooms. May I sit?"

Herod reclined at the end of the large table laden with fruits and nuts, vegetables, cheeses, boiled eggs, dried fish, sliced meats, and delicate pastries. The rest of his party followed suit, and when Herod helped himself to the refreshments they did likewise.

Kissing the crumbs from the ends of each of his fingers, Herod turned to Pilate.

"Tell me; what is the news, my brother?"

Pilate shrugged. "I have no complaints. The taxes have been collected without incident. I am doing some renovations to my palace, which should be complete by the summer. And you, how are you, Herod? You seem to have put on some weight."

Herod patted his pot belly merrily and said with a devious laugh, "Oh, you know the good life. Eat, drink, and be merry, for tomorrow we may die. Speaking of death, I hear you are having a problem finding a dead body. There are all sorts of rumors in the streets. I have even heard that your own ability to rule has been called into question. Have you heard these rumors?"

Pilate stood erect with his hands folded behind his back. He intentionally walked to the window without saying a word. After gazing out at the city, he turned toward Herod and smiled, making his way back to his original position.

"No, I have not heard these rumors. Maybe you will inform me of the rumors that are in the streets." Pilate shrugged again, as if the rumors were not an important topic.

"Of course, my brother, I count it as my duty to assist you in your time of trouble." Herod smiled wickedly. "Could you imagine the embarrassment if Rome were advised that a rebellion occurred in your jurisdiction? And that it occurred over the incompetence of your subordinates? I know it's not your fault that a dead prisoner was stolen from your guards, but you are the one in charge," and Herod waggled his finger at Pilate as if Pilate were a naughty child.

"And think of the audacity of these rebels. They stole the body in spite of the Roman seal upon the tomb!" Herod feigned incredulity. "Your Roman seal meant nothing to the thieves. What might that say about your authority? Not to me, of course, but to others."

Herod sighed. "You see, my brother, I also had a similar problem. It was just about a year ago. There was this nuisance of a man named John the Baptizer. His people looked upon him as a great prophet. I found him interesting. I believe he was related to your missing dead prisoner. In any event he was constantly disrupting the peace of my provinces with his moral condemnations. He accused me of some kind of lustful wrongdoing." At this, the entire party around the table broke into gales of laughter. "Well, my patience wore thin, and I had him put to death. But I did it right. The way I did it made it impossible for rumors to spread. I had him beheaded. And I gave him to his followers without his head. You see, Pontius, no room for rumors or speculations. I made it clear to all that I am the power, and no one will usurp it from me."

Pilate waved his servants away as he reached for his own drink. While pouring wine into his cup, he stood and turned toward Herod. Without physical movement or emotion, like a cobra ready to strike, Pilate responded, "That's an interesting story. Did you make it up yourself?

I recollect a very different tale. I recall that John the Baptizer accused you of many wrongs. I believe he accused you of sleeping with your brother's wife. Isn't that unlawful for you, as a Jew?" Pilate's face folded into its angry frown, and Herod found himself staring into the flinty black eyes. "And isn't it a fact that you feared the multitude because they regarded him as a prophet? Isn't that why you allowed him to continue in his ranting? And wasn't that causing many disturbances in your province? And isn't it true that during one of your perverted parties that the daughter of Herodias danced before you? And in your mindless state did you not promise her anything she wanted? And did she not ask for his head on a platter? Isn't that the real story?"

Pilate paused, but he never took his eyes from Herod.

"In fact, rumor has it that you thought Jesus was John the Baptizer raised from the dead. And you were frightened. Isn't that true?" Pilate bared his teeth. "Now if you imply that I have shown weakness, I would remind you that you also had a part to play. Did I not send him to you? Was he not a Galilean? Do you not have authority over that district? You might want to reconsider whatever it is you are up to."

Snapping his fingers at his entourage while scrambling to his feet, Herod said, "My dear brother, um.. .we must leave. I have many important appointments that I must tend to. I certainly support your investigation and will do everything in my power to assist you. You must come and visit me. I will set out a feast fit for the great Caesar himself."

As Herod hurried from the room, threatening to ruin his dainty slippers, Pilate murmured to Demetrios, "Do you think he smelled blood?"

"If he did," replied Demetrios, "it was his own."

"Yes, it was, wasn't it?" And Pilate sat back in his chair, satisfied that the decadent tetrarch of Galilee was no danger to him.

Three Become One

Underneath the main structure of the garrison were rooms used for storage, but others were used for holding cells and torture chambers. Marcus ordered Anthony forward to prepare one of these rooms for the interview of the temple guard. He explained to his partner that he needed to make the interview environment as dismal as possible.

Marcus then stationed several of the soldiers from Pilate's contingent outside the entrance to the garrison. He assumed the temple priests would arrive sooner or later, and he ordered the soldiers not to allow the interview to be interrupted under any circumstances. He ordered the rest of the soldiers to accompany him inside. He would station them outside the interview room to ensure no chance of escape for the prisoner.

Marcus kept looking about, even turning his body at times, in expectation of a confrontation with the captain of the garrison. But there was no sign of the man, and Marcus and the soldiers did not encounter any problems.

At the foot of the staircase leading to the underground, Marcus was met by Anthony holding a torch. The tunnel-like hallways and inner rooms of the cellar were dark, and the room to which Anthony led Marcus and the soldiers was pitch-black and smelled of burnt flesh.

Within minutes the prisoner was led into the room by two soldiers, whom Marcus dismissed. Anthony locked Saul's ankles and wrists into the tight shackles attached to the wall with heavy chains. Then the two interrogators stepped outside the room and closed the heavy wooden door.

Three soldiers flanked each side of the door, so Marcus and Anthony walked a short distance away in order to discuss their interview strategy without being overheard.

Using hand signals, Marcus let Anthony know that they would begin with the good soldier/better soldier method. Marcus would begin the interview in a firm but gentle manner. Anthony would follow suit, and they would implore Saul to tell the truth.

Marcus whispered, "If I decide this is not accomplishing the goal, I will switch to the good soldier/bad soldier method." And with more hand signals Marcus indicated that Anthony would be the good soldier, who is only interested in the well being of Saul, and Marcus would be the bad soldier, who is ready to take the prisoner's life in order to get to the truth.

The two men discussed at length the many possible scenarios. Finally comfortable with their roles, they reentered the dank chamber, lit only by Anthony's torch. Saul's body shook visibly with fright, and Anthony was reminded of a rabbit Tiberius had recently caught with his own trap. The rabbit had made an excellent stew.

"Saul," Marcus began, "I think we got off on the wrong foot. Let us start from the beginning. Explain to us what you witnessed the night the body went missing?"

Through chattering teeth, Saul responded, "I was s-s-stationed at the tomb for s-s-security purposes. I was ordered by my superiors to keep a close watch on the tomb. The temple priests were concerned that Jesus' disciples were going to return and remove the body. I stationed myself several yards from the entrance of the tomb and kept watch."

Saul rested against the rock wall. The wall was cold, and his trembling increased.

"I-I-I must have fallen asleep. When I awoke, th-th-the rock that was in front of the tomb was moved. I approached the entrance of the tomb and peered in. I noticed the grave clothes but no body. I shouted to the other guards who were also asleep. We all realized that the disciples had stolen the body. I immediately reported this to my superiors. I'm not sure what they did with the information, but they ordered me to return to the temple and to speak to no one concerning the incident. They said that they would explain the facts to anyone who inquired." Saul drew in a deep breath and attempted to still his shaking. "That is all I know."

Marcus looked at Anthony then turned to Saul.

"Saul, there are too many inconsistencies in your story. I realize that you feel like you're caught in the middle of this mess. And, in fact, you are. But it doesn't have to be this way. You see, we have information from other sources that contradicts your statement. We are not interested in getting you in trouble with your superiors, but at the same time we are obligated to uncover the truth and report our findings to our superiors. I'm sure you understand that they can be very brutal if they think they are being deceived. So why don't we start again?"

Unexpectedly, Anthony announced that he was hungry and suggested that he bring back food. Marcus was dumbfounded, but when he was alone with the prisoner he perceived that Saul wanted to change his story but was apprehensive.

"It is in your own best interest to tell the truth," urged Marcus. "Rome will not hold you responsible or liable for the missing body. However, we will take action if you lie."

Anthony re-entered the room and placed bread and wine on the table. The two interrogators broke off some bread and passed the bottle of wine back and forth. When only a small amount remained, Anthony carried the bread and bottle over to the prisoner. He held the food to Saul's mouth and said, *eat.*"

Saul looked at Anthony in wild-eyed amazement, but he did not hesitate to seize the bread with his teeth. Starving prisoners was routine treatment, and Saul could not know when he would be offered food again. When Anthony tipped the bottle against his lips, Saul gratefully gulped the wine.

When the bread and wine were gone, Marcus said, "Once more, Saul."

"You don't understand," said Saul. "I am Jewish. I have no authority. The temple leaders have all the power and authority over the Jewish community. If I were to contradict them I would be excommunicated. I would have nowhere to turn. My family would be ostracized. I would not be able to provide for them or for myself. This may seem like a simple matter to you, but it is life-altering to me. I cannot change my story."

Anthony and Marcus stared at Saul for several minutes. Saul gazed down at the floor and would not lift his eyes. With an inclination of his head, Marcus indicated to Anthony to follow him out of the room.

Once again the men evaluated their strategy. They concluded that neither planned approach would work. Marcus decided the interview technique that would prove most effective would be the bad guy/worst guy method.

"My patience has grown thin, and I can see that you are frustrated," whispered Marcus. "We will beat it out of him if we have to."

Anthony stormed back into the room and began slapping Saul about the head.

"Listen carefully, you pig. Your story is worthless. It is inconsistent and an outright lie. You expect us to believe such nonsense? You fell asleep? What kind of idiots do you take us for? You pig, you're going to talk, or I will make sure that you'll never talk again." Removing his sword from its sheath Anthony continued, "I'll cut your tongue out right now if you don't start talking. And I want the truth. No one could sneak up to that tomb without being overheard. No one! No one could have moved the rock from its place without alerting you."

Pushing the point of his sword into Saul's chest, piercing his tunic and drawing a thin line of blood, Anthony roared, *Start talking!*"

Saul sobbed. "You won't believe me if I tell you the truth. Why don't you get the information from your soldiers? They witnessed the same event. They have nothing to lose by telling the truth. I will lose everything

I've ever acquired. Please, I beseech you, show mercy to me!"

Anthony moved the point of his sword from Saul's chest to his throat. Saul whimpered, and then began to stare into space…"You want the truth? I'll give you the truth."

Immediately, the men observed a dramatic change in the prisoner. The convulsive shaking disappeared. His face smoothed, and his posture straightened. In a very low voice, Saul spoke, "I'm not afraid anymore. My life is over, but so is yours. How are you going to explain this event to your superiors? They will want to execute you after you report to them what I say."

Marcus and Anthony exchanged looks. Saul's eyes had attained a distant cast.

He said, "No one slept. I heard your soldiers talking throughout the night. They stood there in uniform with their shields and their swords. They ignored me as if I weren't there. That's standard procedure from those arrogant swine. So, we were all there, keeping an eye on the tomb. After the Sabbath, as the sun began to rise on the first day of the week, a severe earthquake occurred."

Experienced interrogators, Marcus and Anthony were convinced they were finally getting to the truth.

"I was a few yards from the entrance of the tomb when the earth shook. It appeared that the stone rolled away from the force of the quake. At that very moment, what looked like a man appeared; he was standing on the entrance rock. He shined like the sun, bright like lightning. I couldn't move. I was so afraid I couldn't move. I couldn't talk, none of us could. I thought I was dead, as if I was standing outside myself.

"Suddenly this man moved off the rock as some women approached. I heard him speak to them, but I don't know what he said. Then he vanished."

"Vanished? You mean he got away?" demanded Marcus.

Saul shook his head hopelessly. "No, no. I mean, he disappeared. Evaporated, like an apparition. Like a ghost."

Marcus frowned. "And what were you doing?"

"I stood motionless and speechless, along with your soldiers. They were in a similar condition. As soon as I was able to move, I ran into the city and reported to the chief priests what had happened. Your soldiers were right behind me. The chief priests assembled the elders. They came up with the story that I originally gave you. They warned us that there would be severe ramifications if we told the story as we had told it to them. They didn't believe us anyway. They suggested that it was the disciples and the reflection of torches in the night.

They bribed your soldiers with a considerable amount of money. They promised your soldiers that they had tremendous influence with Pilate, and they need not worry. Your soldiers were concerned by the fabricated story because of the consequences of sleeping on duty, but the chief priests convinced them that our original story would cause more problems for them. The priests convinced the soldiers that their testimony would certainly be viewed with great suspicion, and they had a better chance with what they contrived. They also convinced them that they would most certainly be arrested and placed in prison for life for such a tall tale. They may even be deemed mad and lose their pension.

Who would believe such a story, the priests insisted. And what of their families; they would be in jeopardy. They finally accepted the bribe.

"I was then ordered to reside in the cellar of the temple until the incident blew over. And that is the truth, all of it."

After listening intently Marcus inquired, "Saul, let's go back a step. Describe the man who appeared on the rock. Be specific."

"I believe it was a man," Saul said quickly. "This… this person appeared to be shining like a bright white light, like lightning in the night sky. His clothes were pure white. I cannot compare his appearance to anything I have ever seen." Saul looked at his interrogators with shyness. "He…he may have been an angel, a messenger from God. They sometimes appear in that fashion, according to our Scriptures. I watched him; he sat on the rock and had a conversation with the women who approached the tomb."

"Did you recognize the women?"

"I believe they were the followers of Jesus. They carried linens and containers of embalming spices."

"Is it possible that this was some kind of hoax?"

Saul laughed derisively. "Yes! Sure! It could have been a hoax! That is, if his followers could make the earth shake, and the rock move, and a bright, white light shine from a human body. And then make that body disappear into the air. Yes, sure, it could have been a hoax."

Marcus stood up in anger ready to strike the prisoner. Instead he gestured to Anthony, and they left the room. Pacing at the end of the hallway, they discussed Saul's testimony. In spite of using hand signals and whispered conversation, the discussion became a heated argument that was drawing the attention of the guards. Anthony was convinced that Saul was telling the truth. Marcus refused to make such an inference.

"When the totality of the circumstances that have already been revealed are considered, the story does seem reasonable," Marcus admitted, "but Pilate will never accept this story. I now understand why the soldiers hoped this incident would go away."

Anthony's eyes had become veiled again, and only an icy glare emanated from the blue depths. Marcus felt abashed by the younger man's contempt, but he could see no alternative. He said, "It may have very well been a reflection of light from the torches of the thieves that were perpetrating this crime. And the guards may have been sleeping so that they thought it was more than it was."

Marcus spun on his heels and returned to the room, effectively ending the debate with Anthony. He stated as he entered the room, "It does seem possible to me that you, in fact, fell asleep and were startled by the theft in progress. Now that you had a chance to reconsider, is it possible that the light from the man on the rock may have been a reflection of torches from the thieves as they were making their escape?"

Saul snickered and smirked. "You see. Now you understand. That is the way it must be. And if you are satisfied with that story, so am I."

"We are not satisfied," said Anthony as he closed the door behind him. "We will only be satisfied with the truth."

Saul frantically swung his head toward Marcus. "What do you want from me? I told you what I saw. Now what do you want?"

Marcus realized he was losing control of the interview and that it was becoming a spectacle to the outsider—a temple guard. He ordered Anthony to release the man.

"This interview is over," he commanded with finality.

Anthony held his tongue. He strode over to the shackles and released the prisoner, who stood rubbing his arms and stamping his feet to restore the circulation to his numb and swollen limbs.

Marcus took Saul by one arm, Anthony took the other, and they made their way back outside to the entrance of the garrison, followed by the six Roman soldiers who had stood guard outside the room.

Returned to the broad light of day, Marcus had to squint against the assault to his eyes after the darkness of the cellar. But when his eyes had adjusted, he saw that his prediction was coming true at that very moment. A commotion was taking place at the entrance to the garrison. The six remaining soldiers stationed there were arguing with a crowd of Jewish elders and priests. They were demanding the release of Saul, their temple guard.

Marcus and Anthony let go of Saul, and the little man ran to the priests.

"He may go," Marcus called loudly. Slowly, with Saul in their midst and everyone speaking at once in hushed tones, the priests turned to leave. Marcus turned to the contingent of soldiers sent by Pilate.

"You, too, may go. We have accomplished our business with the temple guard."

The leader of the unit bowed his head to Marcus, snapped his heels, and the contingent marched off. Just then, another contingent of soldiers rode up on horseback.

"Say there," the leader of this unit called out, "do you know where we might find Marcus, the investigator?"

"I am he," Marcus responded.

With that, two of the soldiers separated themselves from the rest and approached Marcus and Anthony. Behind them, the leader said, "These are the two soldiers who were stationed at the tomb of the missing man. Pilate ordered us to retrieve them from Joppa and return them to you."

"Very good," said Marcus. The two men bowed their heads in each other's direction, and then the rest of the horsemen swung around and headed back in the direction of Pilate's palace. To the two remaining soldiers, Marcus said, "Go, and get something to eat. Stay there until we come for you."

As the soldiers turned their horses in the direction of the dining hall, Marcus began walking alongside Anthony in order to debrief on the interview with Saul.

However, before they could begin, they were interrupted by a thin, hoarse voice.

"Excuse me; may I have a word with you?"

Marcus and Anthony noticed a lone priest, still standing off to the side. He had apparently been waiting for an opportunity to speak.

"My name is Nicodemus. I was advised that you were searching for me."

"Nicodemus, yes," said Marcus. "We were attempting to locate you. I'm sure you have heard by now of our investigation regarding the missing body of Jesus. We have been provided information by your colleague Joseph of Arimethea in reference to your part in the removal and subsequent burial of Jesus. From Joseph's testimony and interviews with many of Jesus' disciples, we have accumulated much information. At this point in time I'm not sure that there is anything you could add to their testimony."

In a tone of great humility, Nicodemus said, "I believe I have something to disclose."

Without looking at each other, Marcus and Anthony drew closer to the elderly man. "Go on," said Marcus. "You have our attention."

Nicodemus glanced around and then said, "As incredible as this may sound, Jesus has appeared in the flesh at least ten times on ten different occasions since you began your investigation. I'm sure you're aware of Mary Magdalene's contact with him at the sepulcher.

"She was one of the women who were met by the angel that sat upon the rock at the entrance to the tomb. This, she told me herself. He also appeared to Mary, Salome, and Joanna as they were leaving the sepulcher early that morning. Later that same day he appeared to Peter, one of his closest followers. He appeared to Cleopas and another disciple as they were on their way to Emmaus. That night, the night of his Resurrection, he appeared to ten of his followers as they were all gathered together in one room."

Nicodemus' eyes glowed brightly, like polished stones.

"They were in a locked room, doors and windows barred; for fear of the Jews, you see. When suddenly

Jesus came and stood in their midst. He showed them his wounds."

"*Enough!*" Marcus shouted, and he raised his hand as if to slap the old priest. "I have heard enough! This makes no sense to me!" And he chopped at the air angrily and impotently with his raised hand.

In a pitying whisper, Nicodemus said, "I know. But I also know this. Jesus' appearances have come in most cases to groups of people, and they all saw the same thing. The disciples have gone back to their occupations, which mean they are stable people, capable of resuming their trades." Nicodemus stretched out his hand and placed it on Marcus's shoulder. "Keep in mind, these men were skeptical too and did not believe until they saw for themselves."

"We are finished," snapped Marcus, and he flung off Nicodemus' hand. "But I would like to ask you one last question. You said that Jesus appeared in a locked room, where the disciples were hiding. If he has this marvelous ability, then why…why would anyone have had to move the rock in order for him to escape?"

Marcus waited for Nicodemus' answer like an eagle circling his prey.

Nicodemus folded his arms beneath his shawl, leaned toward Marcus, and said softly, "*So you could get in.*"

Marcus was stunned by the answer. The magnitude of Nicodemus's solution was not lost on Marcus. Standing beside Marcus, Anthony felt his entire being vibrate with excitement.

Marcus backed away from the elderly priest, and then hurried toward the garrison. Anthony smiled uncertainly at the priest and then followed Marcus. As he caught up to his partner, Anthony asked, "Would you like me to follow up on Nicodemus' report? I could round up those people who have reported seeing Jesus since—"

Marcus thrust his face into Anthony's until they were nose to nose and aggressively said, "Haven't we determined that Jesus is dead?"

Resuming his march to the dining hall, he barked, "Focus on the task at hand. We have two Roman brothers to interview, and their testimony is paramount to this investigation. I believe it would be in our best interest to interview them separately. I'm sure by now they understand the implications of their first statements. It may be difficult for them to change their story.

"They are probably still counting on the influence that the priests have with Pilate. Either way they have placed themselves in a very precarious situation. If they stick with their story they have sealed their fate. Pilate will have their heads. If they change their story they would have to admit that they have committed perjury, and their original testimony becomes a disloyal act against Roman authority. We must use all of our abilities and charisma to influence them to testify truthfully. We must play one against the other. That means we will do whatever it takes to get to the truth. *Whatever it takes!*"

"Don't you think when Pilate hears the truth he will understand why they fabricated their story?"

Marcus again drew his face level with the younger man. Harshly, he said, "First of all, Anthony, obviously you have been bewitched by these Jews and have concluded that something spectacular has occurred. I have not. Furthermore, you are speculating on what Pilate's reaction will be. I told you before, he is a politician. He is not interested in the truth. His only concern is for himself, his power, and authority. And if he perceives that anyone is placing him in a dangerous position he will eliminate the threat. People have disappeared in the darkness of night. Don't be naive concerning your rights or anyone else's rights as a Roman citizen. They don't exist." Marcus stepped back and ordered, "Go and retrieve the soldiers. Separate them into private rooms and wait for my arrival. I have some business to attend to; when I'm through, I will join you."

Anthony continued toward the dining hall, but at the doorway he looked back toward Marcus and saw that he was speaking with a unit of four soldiers. He observed that they were gazing at him as Marcus spoke. He wondered what that conversation was about. He was familiar enough with Marcus's ways that it appeared to him Marcus was directing them to a task, but what task? And what did it have to do with him that they were looking at him so intently?

In the dining hall, Anthony got a plate full of food and joined the two soldiers at their table. He learned their names were Gracchus and Justus. They seemed curious about their recall from Joppa for an interview regarding the dead man Jesus, but they did not seem unduly concerned. The three men bantered about life in the godforsaken desert.

When he had finished eating, Anthony led the men to the cellar of the garrison and placed each man in a separate room, seated at a table. He then waited for Marcus again in the torch-lit hallway.

When Marcus entered the first room with Anthony, he was somewhat dismayed to see Gracchus seated comfortably at a table. He would have rather been face to face with the witness, which is much more intimidating. However, it was incidental at this point.

Anthony began, "Gracchus, we have been commanded by Pilate to investigate the missing body of Jesus, which you and others were ordered to secure. We have completed our investigation at the tomb and have interviewed many witnesses. We would like you to explain what happened that morning. I want to emphasize that we have ascertained pertinent information, and it is important for you, at this time, to be truthful."

Gracchus's hands betrayed a slight tremor, and a muscle worked in his jaw. Otherwise, he maintained his composure as he explained to the two investigators that he had been ill prior to the crucifixion of this prisoner Jesus, and because his body was weak he had fallen asleep.

"I made a grievous mistake," he said, "and when I awoke his disciples had stolen him away."

"Gracchus, Gracchus, Gracchus, I asked you to be truthful, and you begin with a lie. And that lie insults my intelligence. Let me explain why. First, you want me to believe that the disciples stole the body. Explain to me how you know that it was the disciples if you were asleep?" Anthony slammed his hands on the table. "Two. Explain to me how anyone would be able to approach that tomb without being heard. Do you have any idea what the entrance stone weighed? How would anyone be able to move that stone without awakening you? I have several other questions, but I'll wait until you answer these. Keep in mind that I don't take lightly to disrespect. And your testimony is a direct insult to our intellect, soldier."

Marcus was pleased with Anthony's interview tactics. He had revealed nothing concerning the facts that they had uncovered. He had made the soldier uncomfortable in his lie. And he had laid out precise questions that a reasonable person would have to consider.

Gracchus returned Anthony's stare as he carefully measured his response. Finally, he said, "My father and his father were great warriors for Rome. My father even fought with Caesar in his great battle against the Gauls. I did not want to bring shame upon my father's name. But I now see that the truth must be told. As the sun was rising that morning, I heard noise in the vicinity of the tomb. I observed several of the disciples removing the body from its resting place. Justus and I confronted the men. The temple guard ran, leaving us to fend off the thieves alone. We drew our swords and fought them furiously, but we were outnumbered three-to-one, so we retreated. I would have stayed and fought to the death, but I thought it foolish to die for the corpse of a Jew."

Instantly Anthony remarked, "It sounds to me that there's not much you would be willing to die for." They both stood simultaneously and drew their swords.

"Make your move, you bag of camel dung," Anthony invited. "I will split your face in two."

Gracchus remained motionless, and Marcus advised him to sit down. Without taking his eyes from Anthony, Gracchus complied.

Anthony sheathed his own sword and angrily continued, "You have no honor. This lie is worse than the first. I informed you that we have thoroughly investigated this case. That means we took special notice of the scene. Again, you mock our intelligence." Anthony brought his knuckles down on the table and leaned into Gracchus's face. "You heard a noise? You struggled to protect the scene? They overpowered Justus and you? They escaped with the body? That's what you expect us to believe? How many battles have you been in? What's the outcome of a battle when the men are wielding swords? What does that scene look like? Are there any deaths or injuries? Is there blood on the scene? The scene of the tomb showed no evidence of any kind of altercation. Furthermore, we have a statement from the temple guard, and I assure you we uncovered the truth."

Alarmed, Marcus felt the blood pounding in his temples. Marcus knew that Anthony still embraced the notion that Pilate would accept whatever the investigation uncovered, and the fantastical discoveries of this investigation could have devastating consequences for the soldiers' careers and reputations in the Roman legion.

Marcus was about to speak when Anthony said, "Gracchus, there are many unexplained occurrences, but that doesn't mean you cannot tell the truth. The truth is always better than a lie. You spoke of your father and his father. I'm sure they are honorable men. They would want you to speak the truth. I promise you that I will assist you by providing the information we have uncovered. You are not alone in what you witnessed."

Marcus stepped toward the table and placed a gently restraining hand on Anthony's shoulder, but Gracchus had been staring down at his hands, and he now spoke.

"I'm a good soldier. My record will confirm that."

Marcus let his hand fall as Anthony straightened up from his bent position. Both men sensed that the interview was going in a new direction—toward the truth.

"That night I positioned myself a few yards from the entrance of the tomb," Gracchus said. "I stood all night, my back up against the rock cliff so that I could not be assaulted from behind. Just before dawn a great earthquake shook the ground. The entrance rock rolled out of its place. Suddenly there appeared a person on top of the rock. He glowed in the darkness." Gracchus looked defiantly at the two men and said defensively, "Justus was a few feet from me and observed the same event. None of us moved, not I nor Justus nor the temple guard. Several women approached. The person on the rock spoke to them. Then this person disappeared. I looked toward the tomb, and I could see the cloths where the body had been; the body was gone.

"We ran back to the city and met with the Jewish priests. They questioned us as to what we had witnessed. They were concerned and anxious. I suggested we leave and report to Pilate what had occurred, but the priests convinced us that we appeared as mad men and that we would lose our positions in the legion. They made a persuasive argument…it was all irrational."

Anthony empathized with the internal struggle that Gracchus described and looked for support from Marcus's demeanor. Gracchus also looked for an indication of Marcus's perspective from his expression. Neither soldier was able to get a read on Marcus's viewpoint.

Gracchus paused, took a deep breath then went on, "They suggested that we should say nothing of what we thought we saw. They told us to testify that we had fallen asleep and that the disciples had stolen him away.

Justus and I knew that sleeping on duty is punishable by death, but they assured us that they could convince Pilate otherwise. They alluded to the treasury that they maintain at the temple, as if they could bribe the governor if necessary. They also argued that Pilate would have no interest in a missing corpse, especially a Jew." Gracchus shrugged and shifted his feet. "It seemed the right thing to do. They handed us money for our trouble. I know it seems as if we took a bribe, but it wasn't like that. They were so convincing."

Marcus could not keep the infuriated gruffness from his voice. "You said that a man appeared on the rock entrance to the tomb. Are you not a soldier of Rome? Do you not have a duty to fulfill your mission? Explain to me why you and Justus did not attempt to arrest, subdue, or kill that perpetrator. I could understand why the temple guard neglected his responsibility, but not a trained Rome soldier who was specifically assigned to do just that. I have no sympathy for you or anyone who wears the Roman uniform and is derelict in his duties. Now, explain your incompetence!"

"I have no excuse, sir. The man…was not…he was different." Gracchus let his voice trail off on a note of frustration.

Anthony nodded his head, and Marcus became more fearful of his partner's empathy for this story. Before he could let Anthony speak, Marcus immediately ordered him to retrieve the other soldier while he escorted Gracchus outside.

When Marcus returned he called Anthony into the hallway, out of earshot of Justus. Marcus explained that he would lead the interview and that Anthony was not to say too much. He informed Anthony that he had conducted a fine interview with Gracchus, but he should not get emotionally involved with the soldiers' circumstances or their fate.

"We are not in control of their destiny," Marcus stated.

The icy glare returned to Anthony's blue eyes as he argued with Marcus.

"It is our responsibility and duty to testify to the truth concerning this investigation. In doing that we would assist the soldiers and demonstrate the rationale of their actions at the scene."

Marcus directed Anthony back into the room with a wave of his hand. He was finding the younger man's stubborn naivete impossible to battle.

Justus waited at attention. He was an older man, worn and weary from his many years of soldiering. Marcus told him to sit and relax.

"Justus," Marcus began, "I'm not going to play games with you. I'm going to be straightforward with you, and I expect the same courtesy and respect in turn. We have just received a formal statement from your partner that corroborates previous testimony from Saul, the temple guard who was also assigned to the tomb. The story of the disciples sneaking up and stealing the body is null and void. In reality we don't even need a statement from you, but we are giving you the opportunity to make this right, if not for yourself than for the sake of your young partner. Why don't you explain to us what exactly occurred on the morning in question?"

"Make this right, you say? For the sake of my young partner? Please; you want me to be truthful, then don't throw that crap at me. I've been around a long time, and

I've heard it all. Let me say this…I've been considering what my testimony would be if I were questioned. I have no illusions as to what the final punishment will be for me; there's no getting around it. However, I do have a request. I request leniency for Gracchus. I was the officer in charge that night. He did what I ordered him to do. He is not responsible for our dereliction of duty and that we ran from the scene. He wanted to make a stand against this…" Justus seemed at a loss for words. "This… this shining whatever it was. I call it a man, but I've never seen a man like that. Gracchus wanted to report the facts as they were to Pilate, but I refused. You have been around, and you know how it goes."

Marcus could not deny the contraction he felt in his heart, but he did not waver in his stance. He waited for the old soldier to go on.

"It's a brotherhood, and we stick together," Justus said. "What Gracchus did, he did for me. I want a guarantee that he is shown leniency. If not I won't cooperate. My testimony may or may not corroborate his story, but you will never know."

"Justus, I will do what I can for you," Marcus said.

Justus inclined his head in a slight bow. He said, "We were stationed at the tomb that night. We had direct orders to protect the tomb from thieves. We were informed that his disciples may attempt to retrieve his body. The night was without incident. Throughout the night we conversed, mostly small talk. I may have periodically dozed on and off. But this type of assignment isn't new to me, so I was very aware of my environment. Early in the morning, just about daybreak, the earth underneath our feet shook violently. I moved away from the rock cliff. I was concerned about falling debris. During the shaking the entrance rock to the tomb rolled about ten yards from its original place. I stepped toward the tomb and peered in. It was dark, and I couldn't determine if anyone was inside. Then there appeared to be a man sitting on the top of the entrance rock. His clothes were bright white, and he shined. None of us moved. I heard people approaching from the opposite direction, women. They stood before the rock and were spoken to by the man. He disappeared. I again looked inside the tomb, which was empty. Only the grave clothes were inside."

Justus paused and looked at Marcus, expecting questions. When Marcus said nothing, the old soldier continued.

"We left the scene and hurried toward the city. We attempted to explain to the elders what had happened. It must have appeared to them that we were hysterical. They suggested we proclaim that Jesus' disciples came and stole the body. I knew then what the issues would be for us regarding our sleeping on duty, but I thought this story sounded the most reasonable. I couldn't imagine testifying to the other. Who would have believed us? Sometimes the truth is not the best answer. The elders persuaded us that they would be able to make an amicable arrangement with Pilate. They then bribed me with gold and considered our business complete. Gracchus refused the bribe so I kept the gold. All along the way to the garrison Gracchus wanted to report the truth, but I convinced him otherwise. I made him promise to keep this to ourselves. When we arrived at the garrison we were ordered to Joppa."

Marcus's greatest concern at this point was Anthony. He could see that he was going to have problems with his partner. Marcus was going to dismiss the guards' story; he felt he had to. So Marcus ordered Anthony to accompany Justus out to the front of the garrison. Marcus followed behind. At the garrison entrance Marcus turned Justus over to a contingent of soldiers who were awaiting his arrival. They already had Gracchus in custody, and now they proceeded to Pilate's palace.

Anthony was bewildered by Marcus's lack of questioning. He asked what would be the outcome concerning their testimony. He hoped their telling the truth might spare them punishment.

"That it is not our concern," Marcus said brusquely, and he ordered Anthony to retrieve the records of the investigation, which were in the pack on Anthony's horse.

"Anthony, I am going to the palace to report our findings to Pilate. I would like you to proceed to your home and stay there until further notice. That's an order."

Anthony was bewildered.

"What do you mean, return to my home? I expect to accompany you to Pilate and make my report. I'm sure when we explain all that has been uncovered we will save our brothers from harsh punishment. Pilate will have to consider the possibility… "

As if Anthony were not even speaking, Marcus turned to a nearby soldier and commanded, "Accompany Anthony to his home."

Unable to contain the fury that had been steadily building, Anthony lunged toward Marcus. The soldiers who were standing by moved as one toward Anthony, and to his astonishment, he realized this had been prearranged. He suddenly recalled the earlier conversation he had witnessed between Marcus and these soldiers.

"You speak of honor?" He spat at Marcus. "You have betrayed me. You have betrayed yourself. We will meet again, and when we do this will be settled once and for all."

With one swift movement, Anthony mounted his horse. The four soldiers surrounded him, and they proceeded on their way. When they had traveled a short distance, Anthony turned for one last look at Marcus, but Marcus was already gone.

Final Report

Using Pilate's seal of authorization, Marcus dispatched two messengers to depart immediately and travel by water with all haste to Rome. He gave them a note to carry to his uncle Hadrian, a senator. The note directed Hadrian to send the best physician in Rome to Judea, using funds from Marcus's own inheritance. The note included specific directions to Anthony's house and a brief description of his son's precarious health, which the physician was ordered to cure.

Marcus then directed two other soldiers to Pilate, with the message that he would see him first thing in the morning. Marcus knew that Pilate was waiting for him, and to keep the governor waiting was bold and perhaps rash. Nevertheless, there was unfinished business to which he needed to attend.

It had been a very long day, and the sun was finally settling on the horizon as Marcus turned his horse toward his destination. Nightfall would bring mostly blackness as the moon was in its most distant phase, but Marcus had gone to this place many times in his mind if not in actuality. He would have no trouble finding what he sought.

As the horse cantered in obedience to the pressure from Marcus's thighs, his thoughts centered on Anthony. He could see the young man's pinched and angry face, the icy blue glare that transfigured into a face of wounded bewilderment. He hoped that someday Anthony would understand the predicament they were in, and that Marcus was only trying to protect him from Pilate's wrath. He knew, though, that forgiveness from Anthony was too much to expect. Anthony would always hold him responsible for failing on the issue of truth.

The truth does not matter. Only survival matters. If the life and death of the Jew proved anything, it proved that, thought Marcus, yet his own thoughts gave him sorrow.

The velvet sky, with its scattering of glimmering jewels, seemed to lower on Marcus when he brought the horse to a standstill.

Before him was the modest home he had shared with his beloved wife. It was wasteful that the home was unoccupied now, but Marcus had not been able to allow others to live here. Before leaving the house for the last time, he had destroyed all but the outside walls. As if the destruction were a bad omen, no one else had taken up residence or attempted to repair the damaged home.

Behind the house, several yards away on a grassy knoll, was where she was buried. Marcus climbed down from the horse and walked around to the site, where he released the reins.

"Go on," he said, "get your fill." And the horse followed Marcus's command, contentedly nibbling the tall grasses around the house.

While the horse ate, Marcus drew water from the well. The bucket, with its long rope, still sat beside the deep well. And the water was still as fresh and cold and delicious. Marcus drank several long draughts. When he was refreshed, he filled the bucket and carried it to the horse.

Finally, he turned his attention to the mound outlined by an oval of smooth white rocks, like a pearl necklace. Marcus remembered setting those rocks into place, carefully selecting each one, aligning them, and wedging them into the soil so they would never move, and she would never be forgotten. The world could never pass by her resting place without acknowledging that she lay there.

He settled himself now on the dew-wet grass outside the oval circle. He placed his hand on the mound and found himself stroking the soft grass there.

"I've come back," he said. "I've come back to talk to you."

Marcus's voice broke, and tears began coursing down his cheeks.

"I am at a crossroads, my beloved. I have been involved in an important investigation. If what I've discovered is true, then you were right all along. And your god is God." Marcus drew a deep breath. "But I cannot embrace this… except to you. Or I will be ruined…my life, my career."

Marcus cried silently for several minutes. Then he said, "There is something else. If this investigation can be resolved…if I can lay it to rest and go on…I may have met someone. You would like her, I am sure. She is of your faith, and kind, and gentle. She puts me in mind of you, yet she is her own woman, a good, strong woman. I would like to rebuild this house and fill it with children. Do you agree?"

Marcus closed his eyes and lay back on the grass. Instantly his heart had flooded with a sense of peace and well-being, and he did not want the feelings to dissipate. He held his breath for as long as he could, then slowly released it and looked up at the night sky. Painted against the backdrop, he saw his wife on the day they had walked along the banks of the Tibers. He had taken her to Rome to meet his family. The visit had gone well, and the future had held so much promise. In his vision now, he saw his wife turn toward him as he lay on the ground. She was smiling as she whispered, *"Marcus, the truth can set you free."*

Marcus closed his eyes again and fell into a deep sleep. He was startled into wakefulness by a loud snort against his ear, and he jumped up to face his horse. He laughed.

"You are right, old fellow," he said, assessing the light of the predawn sky. "It's time to get up."

Marcus pulled Anthony's report from his bag and reviewed it. Just as he had suspected, Anthony's report would have been considered treason. Marcus hid those notes back in his bag and rewrote a summary of the events. He then mounted his horse and returned to Pilate's palace.

• • •

Outside the palace, Marcus noticed an unusual amount of activity. He secured his horse and proceeded to the front entrance where he was met by Demetrios and several guards. He recognized one of the guards.

"Felix, what are you doing here? Aren't you stationed at the garrison under the command of Herod now?"

Felix sighed and said, "Yes, but I have been commanded with other soldiers to report to Pilate."

Before Marcus could ask another question Demetrios motioned for Marcus to follow. Marcus could feel the heavy tension in the air as he was accompanied by the numerous soldiers to Pilate's Judgment Seat. He knew this display of muscle was not a good thing for him. And as he approached the governor he could see the scowl that covered Pilate's face. Marcus stopped before him and bowed deeply.

"Glad you could make it!" Pilate bellowed sarcastically. "Everyone else returned last night, but obviously that would have inconvenienced you. I'm sure you were not concerned with my being inconvenienced, were you?"

Marcus opened his mouth to reply, but Pilate held up his hand for silence. The governor said, "I have interviewed the soldiers Gracchus and Justus myself. They had a very interesting story. I'm sure you are aware of it."

This time, Marcus made no attempt to speak. It was evident that Pilate was now on stage, and Marcus was going to be made the spectacle.

Pilate frowned as he noticed the absence of Anthony.

"Where is your comrade, Anthony? I was expecting him to accompany you."

"I detached him from this investigation, Your Highness. I was not pleased with his performance. He was a constant nuisance. He was continually insisting on reporting back to you for your input, but I had other priorities. He was distressed because he believed that I was not conducting a proper investigation. He felt that I was too easy on the Jews that we questioned. So I relieved him of duty and had him escorted away."

"Marcus, Marcus, I think the boy was right. You were ordered to keep me updated. Instead, my soldiers return with two key witnesses, and the head investigator is nowhere to be found. I had to conduct my own inquiry. As if I have nothing else to do. Are you aware of their testimony?"

Pilate stood from the seat and marched toward Marcus, still talking.

"Gracchus began telling some story, which anyone with common sense could identify as a lie. He reminded me of you. An arrogant, cocky know-it-all. Because I am a merciful leader I gave Justus a chance to testify. He appeared sincere and anxious to tell the truth, at least that's what I presumed, but his story was more fantastic than Gracchus's. He swore by the gods that he never slept that night, and a great earthquake shook the ground. And a glowing man stood upon the entrance rock, which had been moved by the quake. I couldn't take that story. In any event, they're *gone.*"

"Gone? What does that mean? They are Roman soldiers and have a right to trial—"

Pilate screamed at the top of his lungs, "You question me? You're going to advise me of their rights? You should be concerned with yourself. There have been several allegations against you, but I will discuss those details later. So then, where is the body?"

Marcus was horrified by his own behavior. He realized that he had blundered exactly as Anthony might have done. He would have to exercise more self-control. He regained the posture of a subservient soldier and said, "I could not recover the body. I conducted an extensive investigation, and I could not determine where the body is. I interviewed all pertinent witnesses that were at the scene of the crucifixion and the tomb, and I could not ascertain the location of the body. As you know, our guards' testimonies were not helpful. Actually, at this point there are more questions than answers."

Pilate's eyes, normally recessed into the folds of his skin, were popping in apoplexy. He looked on the verge of bursting.

"How dare you speak to me with such rudeness. You are a hopeless and incompetent investigator. Give your report to Demetrios."

The servant stepped forward to take the report that Marcus held in his hand. He placed it on Pilate's desk a few feet away and resumed his position near Pilate's seat.

Pilate began pacing with his hands clasped behind his back. Occasionally he would pause to fire his tirade at Marcus or to rub his hand along his jaws.

"Marcus, you have a bit of a problem. It appears that you have broken many of our laws while conducting this investigation. If you have not noticed, there are several of Herod's soldiers awaiting the outcome of my interview with you. These men that surround you are a tribunal I put together myself. If you know what's good for you, you will keep your mouth shut while I inform you of the charges.

"Allegation number one: while conducting an investigation into the missing corpse, you assaulted a senior officer by beating him about the head. You caused extensive physical damage to him, whereby he had to seek medical attention and has been confined to bed rest until this very day. The most extreme sentence, if found guilty, would be death. I'm sure you know that!

"Second allegation: while conducting said investigation you grievously assaulted a temple guard, who is under the authority of Herod. After he was released he apparently died of head injuries. According to the chief priests he died when he returned to the temple. Our medical doctors examined his dead body, at the request of the priests, and they reported that he had some bruising to his face and body, as well as a fresh cut from a blade on his chest. The cause of death was a cracked skull."

Marcus showed no emotion. He peered surreptitiously at the faces of those who surrounded him. They all stared straight ahead, except for Felix, who was looking directly at Marcus. There appeared to be resolve and low smoldering anger in his eyes. When their eyes met, Marcus detected that Felix was ready to come to the investigator's defense. Marcus acknowledged the soldier's loyalty with a barely concealed half-smile and shook his head.

"Allegation number three," Pilate continued. "During the course of your investigation it was reported that there were at least three Galilean women at the scene of the crime the morning the body was stolen. To my knowledge they have yet to be arrested, which is a dereliction of duty. Why would you not arrest the only real suspects who have positively been identified at the scene? I have many more questions regarding the handling of this investigation. I'm sure you are aware of the gravity and seriousness of these allegations. These must be dealt with. I'm sure you can imagine what my judgment will be."

Just then two soldiers entered the room. They apologized for the interruption and requested a private consultation with Pilate. He permitted them to approach, and they began whispering and looking toward Marcus. Pilate's face flushed with anger, and he nodded at Marcus.

"Very shrewd, you are, Marcus. Very shrewd, indeed."

Pilate then dismissed the two soldiers. Looking toward Herod's squadron, he commanded, "Inform Herod that I will take care of this problem. Marcus is under my jurisdiction, and it will be done as I see fit."

When the room was empty and only Pilate, Marcus, and Demetrios remained, the governor sat back down in the judgment seat and requested Marcus's final report on the investigation. The servant retrieved the report from the desk, and Pilate reviewed it while Marcus stood at attention. Marcus wondered what the soldiers had disclosed that had resulted in such a drastic change in Pilate's demeanor.

After several minutes Pilate declared, "This report seems incomplete. How much time have you wasted? Days! Weeks! Do you know? Do you care? You have interviewed witnesses, and this is all you have uncovered? You could not come up with a satisfactory conclusion. You leave many unanswered questions. What do you have to say for yourself?"

"Your Highness, I have no reasonable explanation. Nothing about this investigation makes much sense. Every legitimate theory that I've come up with cannot be sustained."

Marcus hesitated, then decided to plunge ahead and allude to portions of the report he had deliberately omitted.

"There were other interviews that I did not mention in my final report. They were interesting; however, not relevant to the crime itself. That is why it may appear to you that I was being slothful. I can assure you that I was not."

Pilate's glare intensified. It was plain to him that the investigator was holding back. There was information he was choosing not to divulge. Pilate felt the familiar dread grip his bowels. He did not believe that Marcus would double-cross him, but what special information had the investigator come to possess and refused to reveal? Pilate contemplated Marcus. He decided to try another tactic.

"Well, Marcus, I'm not sure that I can assist you with your troubles. You have indeed failed. And so has your partner, Anthony. What a shame. He appeared to be a very honorable young man. And yet I have received word that he has displayed a sympathetic ear to this Jewish fabrication of a risen king. Do you think, Marcus, that if I were to summon him before me that he would dispute this claim?"

Pilate was instantly gratified by the apprehension that settled in the lines webbing outward from Marcus's eyes. He finally had Marcus where he wanted him.

In a tone of conspiratorial confidentiality, Pilate said, "You know, Marcus, many a great warrior has had his turmoil, his failures. Do you know what the great men of the past did when they brought dishonor to the empire? The only honorable thing to do when one has failed his duty."

Pilate's eyes latched onto Marcus's, and then he allowed them to slide to Marcus's sword, hanging at his side.

"In doing so, they secured their inheritance and their family's name. I believe in some cases they even secured the life of their friends. Do we have an understanding?"

Pilate rose slowly to his feet. He had made his decision.

"Now then, I am going to schedule another tribunal. Demetrios, note it for three weeks from today. That will give you time to prepare your defense, and, as if I don't know, time for your uncle to arrive from Rome. Unless he is traveling overland, in which case it will be some five weeks before he gets here. That will be too late. Let us hope he books passage on a ship.

"I look forward to seeing Hadrian; it's been a long time. As you can see, I am showing great mercy again. I have allowed you a way out of this execrable situation. There is still a way to save you and your partner. I will not arrest you before the hearing. You may take your leave and put your personal matters in order. You are dismissed."

• • •

It was evident to Marcus, as he rode away from the palace, that the soldiers had come to inform Pilate of Marcus's use of his seal in dispatching the messengers to Rome. Pilate had incorrectly concluded that Marcus's letter to his uncle was a request for his personal assistance in a legal defense. *At least it caused him some aggravation,* thought Marcus, *and bought me a little more time. Now, I think I'll buy myself a drink.* And he turned his horse in the direction of the nearest inn.

• • •

Anthony and the unit of four soldiers rode all night and arrived when the sky was its blackest, just before the first rays of dawning light would shoot over the horizon.

The escorting soldiers knew that this was an internal problem between Anthony and Marcus—not a criminal sentence—so they treated Anthony with courtesy. They decided to station themselves inconspicuously in the neighborhood and to stay just a few days, until Anthony's indignation had cooled. They had actually enjoyed Anthony's camaraderie on the road, and as the five of them now approached his house, the escorts bade Anthony farewell and went to rest in the stable until the sun put in its appearance.

Anthony quietly entered his home and was surprised to find Madelyn sitting by an oil lamp. She flew to him and clutched him to her in a fierce hug. She slowly released him but would not stop touching him, as if to reassure herself he was real. She had so longed for him to appear that she wondered if she had conjured him.

Anthony saw the well of tears in his wife's eyes, and he knew that Tiberius was ill again. He gently kissed her, feather touches all over her face. In between kisses, he asked, "Have you not been sleeping?"

She shook her head.

"Sometimes I can rest during the day, when Ruth and Rachel are about. But he has such difficulty breathing. It is much worse at night. And I cannot bear it. I cannot sleep; I can't even close my eyes, while he struggles for air."

As she whispered Anthony could hear the labored breathing of the boy in the next room. Tiberius suddenly erupted in long, loud, raspy coughing and gasping. Both Madelyn and Anthony froze, but the fit subsided.

It was now Anthony's turn to cling to his wife. He held her against his chest and rested his chin on top of her head. He did not want her to see him weep, but he was powerless to stop the tears. All of his battered emotions, the result of the investigation and Marcus's cruel behavior, flowed down his cheeks, along with the pain he felt for his son.

Madelyn heard the sobs breaking in Anthony's chest, and she stroked his back. She waited until the worst had passed. Then she ran her hands down her husband's long arms, took him by the hands, and led him to their bed. She would comfort him now as no one else could.

Anthony rose the next morning when the sun was halfway to its zenith. Madelyn had been keeping a close check on him, so she was prepared with breakfast as soon as his eyes were open. She came in bearing a tray.

"What's this?" Anthony sat up and kissed her deeply and gratefully. "As if I were a king."

"You are the king of this house," Madelyn declared.

"Then I have something for the queen," said Anthony, and he reached for his shirt on the floor. From inside the pocket he produced the little glass flask of perfume.

Madelyn's eyes widened in surprise, and her smile filled Anthony with pleasure and delight. But it was his turn to be surprised when she threw her arms around him and knocked him back on the bed. With an aching hunger, they covered each other with kisses; and the tray on the floor may have been forgotten, but a noise in the hall made them go still. They heard Tiberius ask Ruth a question. They quickly looked at and said at the same time, "*Tiberius!*"

The boy appeared at the door.

"Father? You're home!" And Tiberius ran to the bed where he was enveloped in his parents' embrace.

Madelyn took Tiberius by the hand and led him to the door as she said to Anthony, "You eat your breakfast. I will prepare Tiberius some hot stewed prunes."

Within minutes Anthony appeared at the table, carrying his tray.

"I have been away from my family for too long. I want to spend every minute with you now."

Tiberius and Madelyn smiled. Anthony watched his son pick at the prunes. He could see that the boy had lost a good deal of weight and was as pale and weak as a newborn goat. His eyes met Madelyn's across the table; after a moment, she looked away.

They both knew their son was worsening.

"Where is Marcus, Father?"

Ruth had entered the room to clear away the plates, and she smiled at Anthony. He understood that her smile was meant to welcome him home, but he saw the inquiry in her eyes. She, too, wondered where his partner was.

Unable to control his temper, he responded with a cutting edge to his voice.

"We will not be concerned about Marcus any longer."

Anthony was sorry to see the hurt and unhappy confusion in Ruth's face and her embarrassment as she hurried from the room.

Anthony shook his head. He didn't want to deal with the topic of Marcus right now. He said, "Let me first tell you about all that we uncovered. Bring Ruth back in here, and her sister, Rachel, too. I think they should hear this."

When everyone was seated around the table, Anthony, with great excitement, gave every detail of the investigation. He spoke as if he were convinced that this Jesus did indeed rise from the dead.

The eyes of the sisters gleamed with unshed tears, and their faces shone with radiant joy. Shyly, they shared that they had gone to hear the teacher speak, and that they had placed their faith in him as the Messiah.

"We were even baptized by one of his disciples," said Rachel.

"We have heard," said Ruth, "that his disciples are now in Jerusalem, awaiting a promise from the Lord. No one knows what to expect, but it is certain to be miraculous."

Anthony felt his heart quicken. He had a desire to go to Jerusalem, to join the disciples. He also wondered about this baptism. But he was an outsider, a gentile, so he kept his thoughts to himself.

Later in the day, while Tiberius slept in the afternoon heat, Anthony and Madelyn went for a walk. She asked Anthony why there were soldiers around their home. Anthony told her of the situation with Marcus, how Marcus had betrayed him.

"I intend to kill him if I ever see him again," Anthony said vehemently.

Madelyn rested her hand on his arm.

"I realize, my husband, that you have been deeply hurt. But unless I'm mistaken I saw his love for you. He looked at you like a father to his son. Could there be a reasonable explanation for what he did? You told me yourself that he has a tremendous amount of experience in these matters. I'm sure there is more to it than meets the eye. Don't be so angry, my husband, it is not good for you. Did you know that Ruth is attracted to him? She said he showed interest as well."

Anthony gently removed Madelyn's hand from his arm and began pacing back and forth, shaking his head in disgust. "Loves me! More than meets the eye! Reasonable explanation! You have no idea…

"I do not wish to speak of him again," Anthony said abruptly. "And Ruth will have nothing to do with him."

Madelyn nodded and began a new conversation. They spoke of all that had occurred in the village while he had been away.

At the garden outside their house, Anthony waved to a soldier and informed him that he would not be reporting for the next two weeks.

"My son is gravely ill," he told the man. "I've not been home in many days, and I need some time with my family. Please inform Marcus. Tell him I will be requesting reassignment when I return."

The soldier bowed his head, and the unit left shortly afterward.

Anthony found himself unable to stop thinking about Jerusalem. After several days, he spoke to Madelyn as they prepared for bed one night.

"I believe I have to go," he said. "I have to see for myself."

"See what?"

Anthony stared into Madelyn's eyes, brown with amber highlights and hints of dark emerald.

"The Lord?" he said, and he was grateful when she did not laugh.

Madelyn did not even smile. Instead, she said with utter seriousness, "You must take Ruth and Rachel. They will want to go too."

Anthony swept his wife into his arms and held her to him tightly.

"You are wearing your new perfume," he said, with his lips against her throat. And he carried her to bed.

Providence

Marcus continued drinking for most of the night. He wasn't much for conversation, so he kept to himself. When his sadness was outpaced by his drunkenness, he paid the innkeeper for a room and staggered up the steps.

Marcus woke with the white hot sun broiling his face. He moved away from the large, open window and found himself facing the wall, which was dirty and stained. The pallet, too, was stained and smelled of urine and old sweat. The filthy blanket he had left on the floor resembled a pile of dung, in color and stench.

His lips were cracked and chapped, and his throat burned with raw thirst. He felt as though he had swallowed a bucket of sand.

When he sat up, his head throbbed and the room spun. He held his head in his hands, trying to stop the spinning. The last time he drank too much, he and Anthony had had a good time. He remembered a lot of laughter and funny stories. Afterward, he had felt a pleasant warmth in his body, and there had been a humming in his ears, like bees in his head, but the sound had somehow cheered him. This time he had been alone and heavy-hearted, and the drinking had only deepened his depression. Waking in a room that reeked of urine and dung made him feel ashamed.

He stumbled to his feet. He had in mind a memory of a place not far from here. There were many trees, and the branches of the trees had formed a canopy above his head. He had rested peacefully in the shady greenness. That is where he intended to go now.

"Hey!" the innkeeper called after Marcus, who was heading to the door. "Don't you want something to eat?"

When Marcus turned his bloodshot eyes on the man, the innkeeper chuckled.

"It'll make you feel better if you eat something."

Marcus shook his head and kept walking. He overpaid a young boy in the stable to saddle his horse for him, and then he headed in the direction of the place he had called his temple.

When he arrived, he tied the horse to a low branch and stepped inside. He carried his pack with him. He wanted to read over Anthony's report one more time. Anthony's report was concise and truthful. He had not missed a single fact in the case. His insights, contained in a section for comments after each facet of the investigation, were sensible, reasonable, and worthy of consideration.

The report was a work of integrity, and it saddened Marcus more to know that Anthony had taken such great care and diligence with this investigation, and the work would never be appreciated. It would never reach the desk of Pilate, let alone anyone in Rome.

The last entry Marcus read was the encounter with Nicodemus. He then closed the report and set it aside. The meeting with Nicodemus clearly exposed the reasons for Marcus's determination to hide Anthony's report and shield the young man from Pilate. Sightings of the dead man walking around, *for God's sake.*

Marcus lifted his eyes heavenward and addressed God, as if he were listening.

"What is your purpose? In all this, what is your purpose?"

Marcus cast his eyes downward, but he went on talking aloud.

"I have suffered enough. It is time to bring it all to an end. And I must do this for Anthony's sake."

Marcus returned the report to his leather pack, and then he dug a deep hole and buried the pack. After stamping down the earth, he rolled a boulder over the site. Marcus then removed his heavy metal armor and woolen tunic. He intended to use his sword and send it straight to his heart. He placed the handle against a rock and rested the tip against the skin of his hairy chest. When the sword was properly balanced, he would fall upon it with all his force.

• • •

"You shall know the truth, and the truth shall set you free. That's what the Master said."

Voices and rushing footsteps.

Two men were coming rapidly down the road. Marcus dropped to his knees and watched their approach. They were in deep conversation and would probably pass right by the wooded area without realizing he was there.

"No lie comes from the truth. Who is the liar? It is the man who denies that Jesus is the Christ."

Marcus recognized the speaker as John, the disciple of Jesus, and the man with him was Peter. They were coming from the direction of the house where Marcus and Anthony had interviewed them, and they were heading toward Jerusalem. From his place on the ground, Marcus realized he was trembling.

John's words were familiar. He had heard them before. He had heard them just the night before, in his dream, and the speaker then had been his wife.

"The Lord knows everyone's heart," said Peter. "Each and every one needs to repent and be baptized in the name of Jesus Christ for the forgiveness of their sins. And receive the gift of the Holy Spirit. The promise is for everyone, even those in distant lands."

"Let us hurry," said John. "Our brothers and sisters wait for us in the upper room."

As the two men hurried past, Marcus felt great rivulets of sweat running down his face and between the blades of his back. How close he had come to ending his life. And what a mistake it would have been, for he was certain that he had been stopped from his task with a divine message. First, from his wife, and now from the Lord's disciples.

Marcus prayed, "God…if there is a God. I want to know you. I have lived my life for myself. All that I have done I've done for my own glory. I have always felt that something was missing, but I could never put my finger on it. I have achieved honor and glory, and yet I find myself lacking. My God, my God, I find myself burdened and in pain. When my most beautiful wife would speak of you I felt a fluttering in my heart. Oh God, if you are…please make it clear. I wish to follow… Show me the way. Forgive me of my sins and direct me in thy path."

Marcus quickly dressed. He had come to a decision. He, too, would go to Jerusalem and seek out the disciples in this upper room, where they were staying. He knew the truth. Now it was time to allow the truth to set him free.

• • •

Several weeks had passed since the crucifixion of Jesus and his mysterious disappearance from the tomb. Through Ruth and Rachel, Anthony had learned more about the sightings of the man who had risen from the dead. He was convinced the stories were true.

It was late at night, and he was too excited to sleep. He and the sisters would leave for Jerusalem before the sun was over the horizon. He lay now on his back with his arm covering his eyes. If he forced his eyes to remain sealed, perhaps he could yet get some sleep.

He felt Madelyn draw closer to his side, and then he felt her lips on his. With a smile, he removed his arm.

"My good wife, I am going to be leaving shortly. Is there anything you need before I go?"

"Yes. I need to remind you of Ruth's feelings for Marcus."

Anthony rolled his eyes toward the ceiling. His wife always seemed to know what lay within his deepest thoughts. He answered somberly, "I must redeem my honor. If I see him, I will need to deal with him about that."

"You will do the right thing. You always have, my good husband." And she began kissing him again.

It was still early in the day when Anthony and the sisters made their way into the city. Anthony was astride his horse, and he was leading a second, smaller horse.

The sisters sat upon the smaller horse. Ruth, the elder, sat behind Rachel, and each sister faced in the opposite way; Ruth's legs were together on one side of the horse, and Rachel's were on the other.

The city was crowded with Jews from every nation. They had gathered for the Feast of Shavuot. Ruth had explained to Anthony that this festival commemorated the revelation of the Law on Mount Sinai, when God had given the Ten Commandments on the tablets of stone to Moses. Shavuot coincided with the spring harvest festival too, so Jerusalem was overflowing with devout pilgrims.

Anthony noticed that there were more soldiers than usual. *Crowd control*, he thought. He found himself scanning faces for Marcus, and when he caught Ruth staring at a band of soldiers he knew she was searching for the investigator as well.

Suddenly Anthony heard his name called. Turning he recognized Felix. He dismounted and extended his hand to his fellow soldier.

"How are you, Brother?"

Felix looked uneasy.

"There are rumors there may be a disturbance today, so they assigned a great number of us to the city. Things seem peaceful now, but you know how quickly that can change." Changing the subject, Felix said, "I leave soon for Rome. I'm being reassigned."

"Oh?"

"Yes. But I'm glad I got to talk to you before I go. I wanted to say I'm sorry about your friend, Marcus. He is an honorable man."

Anthony felt his head snap back as if he'd been hit.

"What do you mean, Felix? What has happened to Marcus?"

Felix recounted the scene at the palace. He concluded by saying that Marcus had not been seen since.

"The man has the courage of a lion, and he must love you like a brother. Pilate attempted to accuse you as well as Marcus, but Marcus kept you out. It's not unusual for these politicians to find a scapegoat for their errors. I don't know what happened to him. When my squad was ordered out of the palace we were all certain he was being prepared for the slaughter. But he stood tall and never wavered."

Anthony heard a small cry and knew that Ruth had overheard. He glanced in her direction and saw that she had covered her mouth with her hands. A look of terror was in her eyes.

"I will make this right!" Anthony exclaimed.

At that moment a hand grabbed Anthony by his shoulder. In a defensive posture Anthony turned.

"Marcus!" Anthony's heart began to race. He was stunned, but he grabbed his friend and hugged him like a bear.

Felix, too, reached out and clapped Marcus on the back.

"Good to see you, sir," he said. Then he walked off to leave the two men to their own discussion.

Anthony spoke a torrent of apologies, and he begged Marcus to forgive him.

"On one condition. You must promise me that you will obey any order that I give. I mean it."

Without waiting for Anthony to reply, Marcus turned to Ruth. He reached for her hand, and when she gave it to him, he turned it over and gently kissed her palm.

"The sight of you has filled me with gladness."

Ruth's eyes were luminous, and her face had taken on a high sheen. Rachel and Anthony politely averted their eyes, but Marcus and Ruth were enthralled with each other.

It was the jostling crowd that finally forced them to move apart. The horses, restless in the throng, began jumping and stamping their feet. Marcus grabbed the reins of the small horse and shouted for Anthony to secure his horse. They then began walking through the street in search of a place to tie the horses.

All around them the multitude swarmed. It appeared that the entire world had come to Jerusalem. People of every hue and size, distinguishable from one another by their dress and languages. The soldiers could identify Arabs, Parthians, Medes, and Elamites; residents of Mesopotamia, Judea, Cappadocia, Pontus, and Asia. There were others from Egypt, Libya, Rome, and Greece.

When there was a chance to speak and be heard above the noise of the hordes, Marcus said to Anthony, "Why have you brought your maidservants to Jerusalem?"

Anthony stared at Marcus coolly, weighing his answer. At last, he said, "We are here as pilgrims, Marcus, all three of us. We believe that Jesus is the Christ, the Son of God, sent for the forgiveness of men's sins."

Anthony could feel his heart pounding, but he said with conviction, "He rose from the dead, Marcus. You know it too."

"I do know it," Marcus replied. "His words have already saved my life once and brought me here to Jerusalem as well. I have been meeting with the Lord's disciples these many days and listening to them tell the good news. That is what they call it, the good news." Anthony's eyes lit with eager anticipation.

"Could you take us to meet with them?"

"Of course. The room is just over this wall and across the courtyard."

Anthony threw his arm around Marcus and squeezed his shoulder.

"Marcus, I'm so glad. I'm so glad for you, you know?"

"Yes, my brother, I know."

Marcus and Anthony secured the horses and helped the sisters dismount. The four of them crossed the courtyard. At the door of the house, as Marcus raised his hand to knock, Anthony suddenly seized his arm in midair.

"Wait," Anthony whispered. "Is it possible… will we meet… "

Marcus shook his head.

"With all my heart, I wish it were possible. But the believers tell me that he ascended into heaven from Mount Olivet, near Bethany. That happened about ten days ago. I was here in Jerusalem then." Marcus shook his head ruefully. "Seems we were always a step or two behind, but no matter. We've caught up now, I think. The brothers are all waiting for the promised gift. The Messiah told them to wait here for the baptism of the Holy Spirit. He said it would happen in just a few days."

Marcus knocked, and the door was opened by a man who greeted him warmly and welcomed them all. Marcus led the way to an upper room. More than a hundred people sat about the floor. Anthony recognized Peter and John, Andrew, James, Mary Magdalene, and Mary the mother of Jesus. They were praying, so Marcus, Anthony, and the sisters quietly found places to sit.

Suddenly there was a sound like the roaring of a mighty windstorm. Everyone looked up at the ceiling, and the house reverberated with the sound. Then, what looked like flames of fire appeared and settled on their heads.

Everyone began speaking at once, but they were speaking in foreign languages; languages they had never known before.

Realizing they had just received the gift promised by Jesus, the disciples jumped to their feet and ran outdoors. To the vast crowds rushing by, they seemed like drunks in their giddiness, and many people laughed and mocked them for drinking too much wine. But many others recognized their own languages being spoken by the believers, which caused amazement and awe.

"What does this mean?" they asked, and a huge crowd began to gather around the disciples.

Peter's booming voice could be heard above all the noise.

"These men are not drunk! It is only nine o'clock in the morning! No! What you see this morning was predicted by the prophet Joel."

Then Peter, standing with the other eleven apostles, explained that these strange events had all been foretold centuries ago. He told about Jesus' death and Resurrection, which were foretold by King David, and the strange happenings now were foretold by Joel and confirmed King David's prophecy.

"God said, 'I will pour forth my Holy Spirit upon all mankind, and your sons and daughters shall prophesy'" (Acts 2:17 NASV) proclaimed Peter, quoting the prophet Joel. "'Anyone who asks for mercy from the Lord shall have it and shall be saved.'"

Peter went on at length, extolling Jesus of Nazareth as the Lord's Messiah.

"Therefore, I clearly state to everyone in Israel that God has made this Jesus you crucified to be the Lord, the Messiah!" Peter cried out.

When the crowd heard this, they were stirred deeply.

"Brothers, what shall we do?" they called out to Peter and the other disciples.

> Peter replied, "Each one of you must turn from sin and return to God. Repent and be baptized in the name of Jesus Christ for the forgiveness of your sins. Then you also shall receive this gift, the Holy Spirit. For Christ promised the Holy Spirit to each one of you who has been called by the Lord our God, and to your children, and even to those in distant lands!"
> Acts 2:38, 39 (NASV)

"Is this for us also?" Anthony asked Ruth. He was referring to himself and Marcus—gentiles.

"It seems so, Master. He has said it is open to all who are afar off. That would mean to all people who desire to repent and put their faith in Jesus."

Marcus knew that Ruth was right. He recalled the first day he had visited the upper room, the day he had hurried to Jerusalem after overhearing the conversation between Peter and John; the person who answered his knock had been none other than Peter.

Before Marcus could speak, Peter had said, "Marcus! I was wondering if I could speak with you?"

Marcus had stared at Peter, and finally he had said, "I'm sorry about how I acted toward you the last time we met. I had no business attacking your character like that."

Peter stepped outside the door, and the two men began walking about the courtyard.

"I deserved that and more. Actually, that's what I want to talk to you about. What one deserves is an interesting subject."

"I'm listening."

"I know you are, Marcus. It is obvious to me that God has his hand upon you. He is the one who has directed you to this place. Much has been revealed to you, more than to others, less than to some. This is how God works.

"From the beginning God initiated a covenant relationship with man. And from the beginning man has broken that relationship. Like an unfaithful wife we tend to look in other places. God has made himself evident in all creation. His power and majesty are revealed by all that has been made. We are all without excuse. Look up, from the stars to the earth, everything points to his glory and greatness.

"In our case we have been privileged to see things that other generations will not. You have uncovered evidence that makes it clear that Jesus was not of this world. But even with all that evidence it will not bring you into a relationship with God. Let me explain why. I know that as a soldier you have pledged your allegiance to Rome. You are under the authority and power of Rome. If you commit a treasonous act you are liable for that act. The wages for treason is death. The law of Rome demands it. In man's world you can't get around it.

"We, mankind, have committed the same act of treason against God. We have placed ourselves on the throne. What is a God King to do? Justice demands punishment. Retribution is, in fact, the heart of justice. And the wages for sin is death, eternal separation from God. However, God in his infinite wisdom made an escape whereby someone else would pay the price, the wages for our rebellion. This someone is Jesus, God in the flesh. The only person who would have the worth, the unblemished life, would have to be God himself. Can you imagine a God who so loved his creation that he gave himself as a ransom for all? This act of God demonstrated his justice but just as important, his mercy. Sending his Son, God in the flesh, to die for us; who could have conceived such a plan? In the fullness of time he did just that.

"Still, one can have all the evidence in the world, and that won't do it. One must carefully choose Christ and surrender his life to him. You must stand down. Step off the throne and submit to his authority. And as a father who embraces his long-lost child so God seeks to love and embrace his long-lost children. You become his responsibility. Submitting to him is much more than just saying you believe. It's a relationship. And just like a relationship you learn to walk and talk together. You never have to be alone again.

"All those questions that have troubled man from the beginning. What is my purpose? Why am I here? These are answered in him. Saving faith is actually knowledge of the invisible. Trusting in the work and hand of God. I can promise you this, God can always be found. In our darkest hour, when our heart is broken and we feel abandoned. God is there. When we find ourselves at the end of the rope he is there."

Marcus had been unable to respond. His heart had felt so full he did not trust his voice to speak. But later he had prayed, asking God to forgive his sins in the name of Jesus Christ; and Peter had baptized him in a nearby pool, one of the many used for washing and bathing.

Just as Anthony declared his intention to be baptized with the thousands of others on this extraordinary day, Marcus observed a familiar figure in the crowd. It was the captain of the garrison, and Marcus comprehended that the menacing soldier was stalking him posed a danger to Ruth and the others. Marcus would have to divert the captain away from Ruth.

Marcus clapped Anthony heartily on the back and said, "My brother, I have already been baptized. And I just remembered some important business I must attend. I will catch up with you and the women later."

With that Marcus disappeared into the crowd.

• • •

Moments later, as Marcus was rounding the corner of the high outer wall, he was struck in the face with the handle of a sword. He immediately dropped to the ground. As he struggled to get back on his feet, he was continually kicked in the ribs and the stomach. He could hear laughter as he was being beaten into unconsciousness. He was then lifted from the ground and thrown against the wall.

The captain held Marcus there and said, "I told you I would have my revenge." He then punched Marcus straight in the mouth and in the face again and again.

Instructed to be on the alert for trouble, Felix was surveying the crowd. Coming upon one Roman soldier beating another one to death was not what he had expected to see.

"Captain!" he yelled. "You're going to kill him!"

The captain turned to face Felix, and Marcus slumped to the ground.

"He was supposed to have done it himself by now. Pilate wanted me to make sure he was dead. I am to bring his body to him and make sure it doesn't disappear like the other one."

Although Marcus was having difficulty staying conscious, he heard every word. He now found himself meeting the captain's eyes. The captain said to him, "Pilate has a letter from you stating, among other things, that your partner conspired with the Jew's disciples to keep the body concealed. He has become bewitched by them and has committed treason against the empire."

Using his hands, Marcus tried to pull himself up against the wall. The captain slammed him back to the ground with another punch in the face. He laughed again and said, "Pilate's soldiers are already on their way to your partner's house. They are going to arrest him and bring him back for trial. He won't stand a chance after your confession."

"You cannot kill a Roman citizen, let alone a Roman soldier, without a trial first." Felix stepped close to the captain. "If he had done it himself, that would be one thing. But you found him alive. We must take him to Pilate alive."

Felix signaled the rest of his detachment for assistance. He reached down to help Marcus to his feet, and Marcus, through his mangled mouth, managed to mutter, "Must find Anthony."

The captain responded, "If they don't find him at home, they have orders to put the torch to his house, and his family will be executed. His wife is quite lovely, they say," and the captain leered. "I'm sure they will have their way with her first."

Both Marcus and Felix looked at the captain in alarm. Felix quickly arranged for his detachment to take Marcus to a holding cell at the garrison, where he was to be guarded for his own safety.

Staring directly at Felix the captain demanded, "He better not get lost, or it will be you who will stand before Pilate. I will be returning to the garrison forthwith."

Felix ordered his men to be on their way. He then went looking for Anthony among the many pilgrims who had followed the Lord's disciples for baptism, according to what Marcus had told him.

It didn't take long for Felix to find the tall, blond Roman soldier among the Jewish pilgrims. He immediately told Anthony what had befallen Marcus.

"You must take these women to my house, Felix," Anthony said, "and I will go to Marcus."

"But," said Felix, and he reluctantly told Anthony about the soldiers who had been dispatched to arrest him.

"Master Anthony," blurted Rachel, "you must go home. The mistress is with child."

Ruth shot her sister a sharp glance and then looked at the ground.

Anthony's eyes appeared to bulge out of their sockets. His eyes darted from Rachel to Ruth in disbelief. He rushed toward Ruth, eyes still bulging, grabbed her by the shoulders, and gingerly turned her toward him.

"Is this true?" Anthony asked her.

Ruth nodded. "She has all the signs, but she made us swear not to tell you until she was certain." Ruth raised her eyes to look at Anthony. "Master Anthony, you must go home and protect your family. But I must go to Marcus. You understand?" She pleaded for his understanding as she issued an order. "Please take Rachel home with you, and let Felix take me to Marcus."

Anthony hesitated for only a second.

"Yes." Turning to Felix, he said, "The woman is right. Take her with you." Anthony then placed Rachel astride the smaller horse, and he said, "Rachel, you have to ride like a man. Fast as the wind. Hold on tight."

And they rode off.

• • •

At the garrison, Felix got Ruth inside to see Marcus by claiming she was his sister who had come to tend his wounds. He then fetched water, oil, and bandages for her to do just that, and except for the guards outside the door they left Marcus and Ruth alone.

Anthony and Rachel galloped as fast as the horses could go. Although not an experienced horsewoman, Rachel had watched Tiberius and even ridden with him occasionally for company. Besides, concern for Madelyn and the boy set aside all other concerns for herself.

As they rode within sight of Anthony's house, he felt a cold sweat break out over his entire body. They could see dozens of Roman soldiers and their horses outside the house, but they could also see crowds of people, Anthony's neighbors, who appeared to be coming and going from the house. As they got closer, Anthony could see that the women were weeping. *Please, God, Please. I love them more than life itself.* Anthony held back his tears.

"*Anthony!*" The neighbors hailed him as he drew up on his horse. They were all speaking at once, and soon Anthony understood that Tiberius was near death. No one mentioned the soldiers, and they were silent. Anthony looked at the leader quickly and then hurried inside followed by Rachel.

The house was filled with more neighbors. There were women cooking and baking bread at the hearth. They all greeted him and motioned toward Tiberius's room. In the boy's room, Anthony found Madelyn sitting on his bed. He made his way to her and gently sat down.

"Anthony," spoke a deep male voice, and Anthony noticed for the first time two well-dressed, prosperous-looking men in the room.

"Allow me to introduce myself. I am Luke, a physician. I came from Rome at the request of Senator Hadrian," and the doctor indicated the other man. "Your son is very ill. I have given him oil of lavender and geranium. It seems to be cooling the fever. Only time will tell."

The senator spoke, "I am Marcus's uncle. He wrote to me, a letter of some urgency, requesting that I send the best doctor in Rome to care for your son. Marcus never asks his family for assistance of any kind, so I thought I should come too and make sure he is all right. We have not heard from him since his wife died."

Anthony nodded and motioned for the men to follow him from the room. In the hallway, he said, "Senator, Marcus does need your help. We have been involved in an investigation, and Pilate is not pleased by the outcome. Marcus is being held now in a cell at the garrison in Jerusalem. You should go there immediately."

"Yes, immediately. And why are all the soldiers here? Do they have anything to do with this?" asked the senator.

"Yes. They are here to arrest me as well."

"Hmmm." The senator stroked his chin while he thought a moment. "I hate to drag you away from your wife and child at this time, but perhaps you should come with me so that we may settle this once and for all. There is nothing more to be done here in any event."

Anthony frowned fiercely at the senator. "I'm sorry, sir, but there is." And Anthony spun on his heel and returned to the room.

The senator looked questioningly at the physician, who shrugged his shoulders. The two men walked back into the little room and found Anthony on his knees by the bedside, with his hands on his son's chest, and he was praying to God. The men waited quietly and respectfully.

When Anthony finished praying, he stood to leave with the men. Staring intently at Madelyn and breathing deeply in order to control his emotions, he gave a soft kiss on her cheek. At the door, he was stopped by his son's weak voice as he whispered, "Father?"

All three men turned back into the room. Luke bent to listen to the boy's chest. He straightened and smiled.

"I don't like sharing credit with a deity, but it seems you got yourselves a miracle."

Anthony held back his tears. "Thank you, Doctor." He shook the man's hand. Then he fell once again to his knees by Tiberius and offered thanks to God. He hugged Madelyn and Tiberius, admonished Rachel in the hallway to take good care of them both.

Hadrian turned to the soldiers on horseback. "Make haste to Pilate's palace and inform him that Senator Hadrian will be arriving shortly. I expect an immediate audience with him. And my nephew better be alive and well."

As they made their way to Pilate's palace, Hadrian was informed on all the specifics of the investigation. Hadrian ordered Anthony to the garrison while he proceeded to the palace.

• • •

In Jerusalem, Anthony was escorted to the garrison by the soldiers while the senator, accompanied by the physician, went to see the governor.

When Felix saw Anthony, he led him to Marcus's cell. "Your friend is in here," he said.

The two friends clasped each other's arms.

"You're a mess," said Anthony.

"No, quite the contrary. I'm much better now, thanks to Ruth." Marcus managed a slight smile in the direction of Ruth.

Anthony could see that the two of them had come to some understanding in the last few hours. He then told them both about the situation he had found waiting for him at home, and each event that had led up to his appearing in the cell while Hadrian and Luke went to see Pilate. With tears in his eyes, he said, "How can I thank you, my brother? You sent for the doctor to save Tiberius, and the presence of both Dr. Luke and the senator may very well have saved my whole family from the soldiers. Now, Tiberius is well. God has made him well, with a little help from Dr. Luke."

They all exchanged smiles.

• • •

Hadrian arrived at the palace and was escorted into Pilate's private chambers. As the men approached one another they respectfully bowed.

"It is a pleasure to see you again. You look well, Senator."

"As do you, Governor. I've observed your building projects. They are quite magnificent. It appears that you have had great success in governing these difficult people. Obviously your ability in the collection of taxes has been both useful and enriching to your providence. And of course that is a direct reflection on you and your skill to administer. If I didn't know better I would have thought that I was back in Rome."

"You are too kind, Senator. It certainly hasn't been easy. I have worked very hard to bring glory to Rome."

They both peered at each other, hoping to avoid a confrontation. Each understood the power of the other, but neither wanted to lose face.

"You know, Governor, I can use my influence to appropriate more funds for your building projects. Your past achievements would make it easy for me to make a case before the Senate. It would certainly be my pleasure to do that. If you're interested, of course. I do believe that one hand washes the other."

Pilate became more at ease. "Yes, that would be appreciated. It would make my life less complicated if I had access to other funds. And I too believe that one hand washes the other." Pilate thought for a moment. "You know, Senator, it's not always easy dealing with certain personalities. And as you know I have always prided myself on being a fair and merciful governor. However, I do not want that mistaken for weakness by my subordinates or other rulers in this region."

Shaking his head in conformation, Hadrian responded, "I wholeheartedly agree. And I assure you that your fair and merciful decisions will not be misconstrued. I promise you, Governor, that your fairness and mercy will be rewarded at the highest level. And if events go accordingly, any accusations made against you by other rulers in this region will be dealt with immediately.

"On the other hand, as you know, my loyalty to my family is second only to Rome. I have always held justice as paramount to all my decisions."

Hadrian turned, gazing out at the landscape. "At the heart of justice is retribution. In fact, there is no justice without it. Therefore if one promises another that mercy will be shown then that is what is expected. Anything else will bring about retribution. That is not a threat; it is a matter of justice. Do we have an understanding?"

"It sounds perfectly clear to me. I think we have an understanding, Senator. I will make arrangements for the release of Marcus."

They both bowed, and Hadrian made his way toward the garrison.

• • •

From the noise in the hallway, they knew that Hadrian had arrived. Marcus stood to greet his uncle.

"Uncle Hadrian, I was not expecting you to come," he said as he shook his uncle's hand and kissed both his cheeks.

"I thought it was time for a vacation. It had been a while since I last saw Pilate. And I have never been to Judea."

The men laughed heartily. Then Marcus said soberly, "The only charge against me that holds weight is my assault upon the captain."

"Yes, Nephew, it does hold weight. I'm sure if we fought this in court we could make a reasonable defense since he has committed the same act upon you. However, I think it would be in your best interest that we just let these events fade into the night." The senator stared directly into Marcus's eyes and continued, "Pilate has decided to drop the charges, and you have decided to thankfully accept his mercy. Do you understand that, Nephew? We are all free to leave, and I know that I have seen enough of this garrison."

"Yes, Uncle. However, there is a part of me—"

"Let it go, Marcus. You must learn to choose your battles wisely. And if you're planning to stay in this region, you do not want this battle. I'm sure there will be others."

• • •

As they approached Anthony's home, the four men on horseback and Ruth riding with Marcus, they saw

Madelyn, Tiberius, and Rachel coming out to meet them with lanterns now that it was nightfall.

"Tomorrow is a new day, Marcus," said Anthony. "New day. New life."

Marcus gazed at Ruth, caressing the arms that encircled his waist. "New life, yes, new life."